THE LIPSTICK MURDERS

An enthralling crime mystery full of twists

ROGER SILVERWOOD

Yorkshire Murder Mysteries Book 25

JOFFE BOOKS

Revised edition 2021
Joffe Books, London
www.joffebooks.com

First published in Great Britain in 2016

ISBN: 978-1-78931-724-4

ONE

Christmas Eve 2011

The sky was as a black as an undertaker's cravat. Snow had been falling in Bromersley in South Yorkshire all day and was still coming down in thick wet flakes.

It was 10.30 p.m., and the doors of Moore and Moore, the advertising agency in an old converted hotel on Inkerman Street in the Old Town district of the town, swung open allowing a brief illumination of the accumulations of the white stuff covering the deserted pavement and road.

Midst laughter and loud boozy calls of 'Good night and a merry Christmas,' a young man burst out smiling and waving. He was carrying a Tesco plastic bag jam-packed full with packets and parcels wrapped in glittering Christmas paper protruding out of the top. He picked his way carefully in the snow through the dark unlit back streets. He was humming 'O Come All Ye Faithful', when the figure of a man unexpectedly stepped out of a house doorway right in front of him.

The young man was startled.

'Got the right time, mate?' the stranger said with a smile.

'Yes, of course,' the young man said and he pulled back his coat sleeve and peered at his wrist.

But he never did tell the stranger the time.

There was a rustle of clothes from behind then the young man felt a mighty blow to the back of the head and a hard fist in the face from the man at his front. The young man dropped unconscious, bleeding on the snow in the gutter.

A third man appeared and they quickly stripped the young man of the presents, his watch, his wallet and the coins in his pocket, then disappeared into the night.

Around the head of the unconscious young man in the gutter the pristine snow was turning pink.

* * *

Four years later
Spring 2016

A man lay propped up in a bed in the Elmdale Private Hospital, Leafy Lane Park, Bromersley, South Yorkshire. His head was heavily covered in bandages. There was a slit in them where his mouth was located, and two short pink plastic tubes projecting from his nostrils through the bandages.

The room door opened and a nurse came in. The man in the bed lifted his hands and arms up into a defensive position in front of him.

'What's that? Who's there?' he snapped through the slit.

The nurse was aware of his nervousness.

'It's only me, Mr Arrowsmith — Nurse Riley,' she said gently. 'Getting everything ready.'

He exhaled loudly and lowered his hands.

She smiled. 'It's your big day today, you know.'

The man was impatient. 'Yeah. I know,' he said. 'It's Monday. What time is . . . How long will it be before he takes them off?'

'It's almost ten o'clock,' she said. 'Doctor Saalheimer usually comes along any time around now.'

Arrowsmith winced slightly.

Nurse Riley looked at him, concerned. 'What's *that* for?'

He breathed heavily. 'Because it hurts,' he snapped. '*That's* what *that's* for.'

She wrinkled her nose. '*Relax now*, Mr Arrowsmith. *Relax*. You need to relax to permit the doctor's work to heal neatly.'

The door opened. A man in a white coat came in.

Nurse Riley turned round and said, 'Good morning, Dr Saalheimer.'

The small man with the bald head and the moustache nodded back at her then turned to the patient and said, 'Ah. Good morning, Mr Arrowsmith. How are you feeling this morning?'

Arrowsmith breathed out heavily. 'I shall be a lot better when I see what you've done to my face, Doctor.'

'Ah yes,' Saalheimer said. 'I think you will be pleased.'

Arrowsmith said, 'Yes. Can we get on with it, Doctor.'

Saalheimer looked at the nurse and nodded.

She turned to a treatment trolley, pushed it close to the side of the bed, put on a pair of rubber gloves, then began to peel off the bandages.

With one hand on the head of the bed, Saalheimer said, 'You mustn't expect too much at first, Mr Arrowsmith.'

Nurse Riley removed the last of the bandage.

Arrowsmith lay still in silence. His face was still covered with a single piece of lint which had holes for the mouth and nostrils.

'I am now going to peel back the lint,' Saalheimer said. 'This may be a little sore.'

Arrowsmith didn't reply. He couldn't speak. He was so close to discovering his new face.

Saalheimer took a pair of forceps from the trolley. He used them to withdraw the short tubes from the nostrils and then to peel back the lint. He dropped the blood-stained lint into the stainless steel bowl.

'Now, Mr Arrowsmith, your face will still be sore . . . and bruised maybe . . . and swollen . . . and red and blue. All those disfigurements will go in a week or two. What I am most concerned about is that your own soft tissue has accepted the transplanted tissue. That is the key issue at this stage.'

Arrowsmith's patience was almost exhausted. 'Just, just . . . do it, Doctor. Do it.'

'I am now going to uncover your eyes. Don't be alarmed. They may take a little while to focus. They have been denied light for so long.'

Arrowsmith clenched and unclenched his hands.

Saalheimer turned round, crossed to the window and closed the shutters so that the room was darker, but there was enough light to work.

Nurse Riley watched closely as the doctor then took away a pad of cotton wool wrapped in lint from each of his eye sockets.

The patient's eyes were closed.

'You can open them now,' Saalheimer said.

Arrowsmith opened both eyes. He blinked several times. Looked round the room. His fists tightened. He began to breathe rapidly. His lips and chin trembled.

'Everything's misty,' he said.

Saalheimer smiled. 'That's perfectly normal,' he said. 'It will be clear in a minute or so.'

Arrowsmith reached out to the lapel of the doctor's white coat, gripped it tight, pulled him down close to his face and said, 'It better had be. Or I'll be the last patient *you'll* ever practise on.'

He then pushed the doctor away.

Nurse Riley's jaw dropped. She leaned back dismayed and looked at the doctor to see how he had reacted.

Saalheimer went scarlet. He inhaled deeply, made himself as tall as he could, adjusted his spectacles, straightened his white coat, crossed to the window and opened the blinds. Sunshine flooded into the room.

Arrowsmith looked round the room, then at Nurse Riley who turned away. Then he looked at the old doctor who also turned away from him with his nose in the air.

Arrowsmith saw the sink, the mirror above it, the trolley by his bedside and the pile of dressings on it. He peered at the dressings. On one of the packets, he could read the words, *Micropore Surgical Tape*.

It was true. His eyesight *was* undiminished. He sighed with relief. A warm glow filled his chest.

Arrowsmith looked at Nurse Riley. 'Got a mirror?'

She glanced at the doctor for his approval.

Saalheimer nodded slightly, and she reached down to a shelf on the trolley, pulled out a hand mirror which she held out in a position so that Arrowsmith could see himself.

He snatched it off her, looked into it and was shocked at what he saw.

'Frigging hell!' he said.

Saalheimer quickly said, 'I warned you about the discolouration, the bruising, and the swelling, they will go naturally, but there are no signs that there is any rejection of the transplanted tissue. That is what is critical, at this stage. Also the invisible stitches, you will note—'

Arrowsmith sniggered and said, 'Yeah. I can see all the twenty-eight *invisible* stitches as clear as day.'

The doctor said, 'I was about to say, that they will be truly invisible in a week or ten days. You have a new face. I need to clean you up a little. That's all.'

Saalheimer turned away, then turned to Nurse Riley and said, 'Saline solution and swabs, Nurse, please.'

She bent down to the lower shelf of the treatment trolley and reached out for a bottle. 'I was certain there was a bottle here, Doctor,' she said. She frowned, stood up empty handed and said, 'The night staff must have used it all up.'

Saalheimer pulled an impatient face. He breathed out noisily.

The nurse's face muscles tightened. 'I'll have to go to the pharmacy,' she said.

The doctor scowled at her and said, 'Yes, well, make it quick.'

'Yes, Doctor,' she snapped.

She went out and slammed the door.

Saalheimer looked after her, shook his head in disbelief, then busied himself at the treatment trolley, cutting up lint to make swabs.

Arrowsmith promptly whipped back the blankets, got out of bed, snatched the fire extinguisher off the wall bracket above the bed head, raised it up and brought it down on the back of the doctor's head. It landed heavily on Saalheimer's skull. The doctor was clearly stunned. He swayed and put a hand up to his temple but still managed to stand.

Arrowsmith's eyes were huge and showing the whites. He lifted up the extinguisher and brought it down again with tremendous force and landed another blow onto the side of the doctor's head. Blood squirted from the old man's right temple and ear. He staggered and then fell onto the floor.

Arrowsmith went down on his knees and checked for a pulse. There was none. Satisfied that he was dead, he stood up, reached into the drawer in the locker at the side of the bed and took out a gold coloured lipstick holder. He pulled off the top, pushed up the red stick, crouched down again and quickly made some daubs on the dead man's forehead. Then he put the lipstick back in his pyjama pocket and pushed the body under the bed.

He stood up and glanced round to see what else he must do. He had to move fast. The nurse may not be long and anybody could come into the ward at any moment. He saw a pair of rubber gloves on the treatment trolley. He picked them up and put them on. He spotted the roll of lint. He took that and wiped the fire extinguisher free of fingerprints before he returned it to its holder on the wall. Then he wiped round all the surfaces he thought he might have touched. He looked round again. His enlarged eyes shone like a frog's.

There was a trickle of blood running out from under the bed. He saw it. His muscles tightened. He crouched down, mopped it up and left the rest of the lint under the bed to stem the flow.

He heard a noise outside in the corridor. He leaped into a position behind the door. It was promptly opened and closed. It was Nurse Riley carrying a large brown bottle. She looked at Arrowsmith standing there in his pyjamas and bare feet. He stared back at her. She saw that he was wearing rubber gloves and that his hands were shaking. She looked away from him as she carefully put the bottle on the treatment trolley. She knew something was wrong. She turned back to face him.

'Mr Arrowsmith, what are you doing out of bed?' she said.

He didn't reply.

Then she noticed the man's eyes staring at her. She suddenly felt very afraid. Her blood ran cold. Her eyebrows shot up. The hair on the nape of her neck stood up. Her lips tightened. She took a step backwards.

'Wh . . . wh . . . where's Dr Saalheimer?' she spluttered.

Looking round the room for some explanation, she saw the small pool of blood created by the trickle from under the bed. She bent down. She saw the body. Her mouth opened wide.

'Oh my god!' she said slowly, with a hand up to her face.

She stood up. Her face was white. She looked at Arrowsmith. His eyes were bulging and unblinking. She backed further away from him. She took in a deep breath to scream.

Arrowsmith swiftly leaped at her. He put a hand over her mouth and the other at the back of her head and pulled her to the floor. He banged her head hard on the parquet floor. She responded by kicking her legs wildly. She tried to yell and to pull his hand away from her mouth. She bit his hand through the rubber glove. He yelled.

'You little bastard,' he said. Ever aware than anybody could come through that door at any second, he quickly moved his knee across so that he was astride her and then he banged her head six times or more on the floor until she was almost senseless and her attack on his hand stopped. Then he grabbed her by the throat with both hands and pressed hard. She made several croaking noises. The muscles on his face tightened. His lips pressed tight back against his teeth. His eyes became bigger than ever. He squeezed her throat even tighter. Then suddenly, she made no more noises. She stopped kicking her legs and waving her arms. Slowly he released his grip. He didn't need to check her pulse.

He pushed his hair out of his eyes, took the lipstick out of his pocket and quickly daubed red strokes on her forehead, then he leaped to his feet, grabbed her hands, dragged her body to the wardrobe, opened the door, took out a suitcase, his suit and shirt on coat-hangers and threw them all on the bed. Then he pushed her body into the bottom of the wardrobe and closed it. Once he got the wardrobe doors closed, he leaned back against them. He was panting. His hands were shaking. He looked at them. He made a conscious effort to take control of himself. He breathed slowly and evenly. He stopped the shaking and stretched upright. He felt more composed. He sighed gently.

And just in time.

The door opened and a young woman in a green uniform pulled a trolley in.

His heart came up to his mouth. His pulse raced.

The young woman looked at the bed and then saw him standing by the wardrobe in his pyjamas. She blinked. Then she walked across to the locker with a jug of water and exchanged it for the jug already there. On her way back she said, 'Tea or coffee?'

He replied without thinking. 'Tea,' he said.

Then he saw a pool of blood on the floor at the side of the bed. It had got bigger. His heart began to thump. He could feel it banging on his ear drums. But he was rooted to the spot. He watched her pour the tea, add milk and sugar, stir it round twice, then carry the cup from the trolley to the locker, then return to the trolley again just skirting the pool of blood. She had passed by it twice. And she *hadn't noticed it*! Or hadn't appeared to have noticed it.

She glanced at him again, and expressionless, pushed the trolley out and closed the door.

He sighed.

He was determined to get out of that room as soon as possible, before somebody more perceptive came in.

He pressed the catches on the suitcase, lifted the lid and took out his underwear, socks, tie and shoes, and proceeded to get dressed. He pulled open the drawer of the locker and emptied the contents into the suitcase. He also cleared the top of the locker of other personal things. He wiped down the top of the locker, and the tumbler with a wet tissue. He tidied the pillows, pulled up the bedclothes, saw the clipboard still hanging on the end of the bed, quickly ripped the notes from it and stuffed them in his pocket. Then he looked round to make sure he had everything. He caught a glance of his face in the mirror over the wash basin. Up close it was a mess. At a few yards it simply looked red and bruised. He would have to keep out of the way for a week or so. He sighed, adjusted his tie, picked up the suitcase and came out of the ward.

He walked briskly along the corridor hoping he wouldn't meet anybody that knew him, then he remembered. Nobody would know him. He had a brand-new face. Nobody in the *world* knew him.

* * *

Her Majesty's Prison, Poulton, Sheffield, South Yorkshire
Tuesday, 8 March 2016, 2.55 p.m.

A large old lady in a big hat, carrying an umbrella with a carved wooden duck's head handle, a large leather handbag and a white paper bag walked up to the main entrance. She reached up and rang the prison bell. A flap opened in one of the big doors and a head peered through. 'Is somebody ringing? Oh it's you Mrs Buller-Price. You're very late today, dear.'

'Yes, I know that Mr Watkins. I've been behind *all* day.'

The Prison Officer said, 'It way past admission to visitors time, you know.'

'My alarm didn't go off, Mr Watkins. It has put me miles behind all day. I knew nothing about it. In fact if it hadn't been for my dogs I would probably still be asleep. I'm afraid I got off to a very bad start.'

'Oh very well. Seeing it's you. But I'm breaking all the rules, you know. I suppose you have a valid visiting order?' Watkins said, holding out his hand.

'Oh yes, Mr Watkins. It's to poor Mr MacBride. Nobody ever visits him.'

He stared at her opened mouthed. '*Mick MacBride*?' he blinked. 'That's because nobody *dare*, Mrs Buller-Price. And he's not poor.'

She passed the official paper up to him.

'I find him a bit reticent but otherwise quite charming,' she said.

He looked at the visiting order, nodded in approval then said, 'Just a minute. I'll open up.'

Seconds later, one of the big doors opened and old Mrs Buller-Price was inside the prison walls.

Prison Officer Watkins walked with her across the quadrangle to the main building and into the hall where a female prison officer patted her down, checked on her handbag, umbrella, and the sponge cake she was carrying in the paper bag, then led her through various doors which she unlocked and re-locked until they arrived at a large hall where fifty-nine male prisoners were already seated at small tables chatting with relatives and friends.

Mrs Buller-Price was directed to one of the tables with a chair at each side. Minutes later, from a door at the other end of the hall, two prison officers escorted a huge man with a face like a pan of spaghetti to the table where she was sitting.

She smiled broadly at him. 'Ah, there you are, Mr MacBride. I'm so sorry I'm late. I expect you thought I wasn't coming, didn't you?'

He sat there like man mountain. He wrinkled his nose and looked down at her.

'Well, you see I'm having such a lot of trouble with the old house, Mr MacBride. I don't know if I told you, but I live in an old farmhouse on the moors my dear father rented from Lord Dingle when he was alive. A lovely man. And the rent was so reasonable. Well, he died and his estate was sold and well, to cut a long story short, the new owners aren't keeping up with their repairs of the house like his lordship did. Anyway, the electricity has fused and everything was off, including my electric alarm clock. I had to get a man in to get me switched on again. He said it needed re-wiring or something. I have approached the new landlord about a leak in the roof, but he was decidedly unhelpful. I'm not sure what on earth I am going to do. It's very costly to keep calling workmen out. You see, I can't really leave the place, I need a house in the country for the sake of my dogs. They must have lots of grounds and fields to play around in. Besides I couldn't go to a house that hasn't got a decent sized garden either. I would die if I had to move and the only place available was a miserable squashed up little house among several hundred other miserable squashed up little houses.'

MacBride glanced round the hall at the noisy, animated prisoners and visitors, some with their boisterous children shouting and crying. Mrs Buller-Price wondered what might have caught his attention, and glanced around to see for herself. She couldn't see anything of particular interest, so she looked back at him.

She recovered his attention by saying, 'By the way, Mr MacBride, I have brought you a Victoria sponge cake. It's filled with some of my home made strawberry jam. I hope you enjoy it.'

MacBride looked at the paper bag and frowned. He tore it open, perceived it was a cake, picked it up with both hands, brought it up to his mouth and took a huge bite out of it. Some of the cream and jam stuck to his cheeks. He chewed it four times and then swallowed. Three more bites and the whole cake had been consumed. Mrs Buller-Price watched him studiously. When it had all gone she pursed her lips, lowered her brow wondering whether he really *had* eaten the whole cake so quickly. Accepting that he must have done, she smiled with delight that he had apparently enjoyed her baking so much.

MacBride then screwed the paper bag up into a ball, used it to wipe the cream and jam off his face and hands, and then put it on the table in front of them.

Mrs Buller-Price picked it up to dispose of later. Then she said, 'I am going to see if I can still purchase an alarm clock that doesn't depend on batteries or electricity. I much prefer them. They're easier to set and never go wrong. Then I will be certain to be awakened at seven o'clock on the dot.'

There was the loud ringing of an electric bell.

She blinked then looked at her watch. 'Oh dear, yes. Times up, Mr MacBride. Oh, and I haven't had time to find out how *you* are.'

He looked at her, frowned but said nothing.

'You can tell me about it next time,' she said. 'And is there anything you want me to bring you?'

Before he had time to ignore her again, two prison officers came up to him. He stood up and walked between them back to the door at the other end of the hall.

Mrs Buller-Price stood up and watched him go. He didn't look back. She sighed. 'Poor man,' she said, and shook her head.

She turned and made her way with the crowd of other visitors towards the door at the opposite end of the hall.

TWO

DI Angel's office, Bromersley Police Station, South Yorkshire
Thursday, 10 March 2016, 8.30.am.

Bromersley's chief of CID, Detective Inspector Michael Angel was at his desk. DS Donald Taylor, the sergeant who headed up the Scenes Of Crimes forensic investigations unit at Bromersley was sitting opposite him.

'We finished examining the scene at the hospital last night, sir, and came away at about seven thirty,' Taylor said.

'And have you got any prints that will identify this chap, Frank Arrowsmith?'

'We found several hair samples, which we assume are his, from the nurse's uniform, and a good amount of his skin samples from under her fingernails. They're on the way to the lab.'

Angel nodded. 'That'll give us his DNA. If he's on the books, Records will show his ID. What about fingerprints and footprints?'

'There are no footprints, sir. And he was pretty canny about his dabs. We looked everywhere, but we got a pretty good set of his right hand from a hand mirror he must have used.'

Angel wrinkled his nose. 'Right, Don.'

'What do you make of the red daubs on both of the victims foreheads, sir?'

'Those daubs seemed to spell out the word *Judas*. But apart from both victims working at the hospital, and operating on and nursing the man Arrowsmith, there doesn't seem to be any other relationship between them.'

'"Judas" implies traitor, doesn't it, sir?'

'Betrayer might be a closer interpretation, Don.'

'Yes, betrayer, sir,' he said. 'It should make it easier to find the mysterious Arrowsmith, sir.'

Angel frowned. 'I hope you are right,' he said, rubbing his chin. 'Judas Iscariot betrayed Jesus by a kiss in the garden of Gethsemane to the temple guards of the Sanhedrin. It's going to be hard to find a close parallel to that, don't you think?'

Taylor rubbed the back of his neck. 'Well erm. Mmm. Yes sir. I suppose it is.'

Angel said, 'Keep me posted.'

Taylor went out.

Angel ran a hand through his hair. After a few moments of thought, he reached out for the phone and tapped in a number. It was to the mortuary at the Bromersley and General District Hospital. Eventually he was speaking to Dr Mac, a respected friend of his who was a forensic surgeon. He was a white haired old Scot from Glasgow.

'Yes, Michael,' Mac said. 'I have finished the post mortems of both victims and there is absolutely nothing that you are not already aware of that could be regarded as unusual or interesting. I will be sending you my full report on both bodies by email later today.'

There was a gentle knock on his office door.

Angel looked up. He cupped his hand over the phone. 'Come in,' he called.

Then back into the mouthpiece he said, 'Right, Mac. Thank you. Goodbye.'

He returned the phone to its cradle and looked at the door. It remained closed.

Angel frowned. Then in a loud voice, again he said, '*Come in*!'

There were a few more seconds delay then he saw the door handle move slightly. The door opened several inches and a small, young face with a lot of black hair and the peak of a police hat peered into the room.

Angel looked at the face, frowned and said, 'Yes, young lady. What do *you* want?'

She hesitated. 'Er . . . erm . . . do you know, please, where I can find a DI Angel, sir,' she said.

'What does it say on the door?' he said.

'Which door, sir?' she said.

Angel's facial muscles tightened. 'The door you're hanging onto, lass,' he said.

The head popped out and then popped in again. 'It says, "DI Angel, head of CID," sir.'

'And who are you looking for?'

Her jaw dropped. 'Oh yes. Oh, sir. Well. It must be you?'

'Yes,' he said quickly. 'Come in. Shut the door.'

It was a very young woman in police uniform. She marched up to the desk, saluted and said, 'PC Cassandra Jagger reporting for duty, sir.'

Angel looked at her and pursed his lips. 'Are you sure you've got the right person, Constable?' he said. 'And you don't have to stand there like Barack Obama in Madame Tussauds.'

She blinked. 'Who, sir?' she said.

He looked down, shook his head quickly several times then ran a hand over his eyes. 'Relax, lass. Relax.'

'Oh,' she said. Then she allowed her shoulders to drop and her feet to have a little space between them to stop her wobbling. 'It was in my letter of appointment, sir.'

'What was?' he said. 'Oh I see.' He held out his hand. 'Let me see it.'

'Yes sir.' She undid the button of a breast pocket, took out a letter in a folded envelope and gave it to him.

He opened it up and read it. He noted that it was on Bromersley force headed notepaper. He looked at the signature. It was signed by Detective Superintendent H. Harker. He might have expected Harker to be behind it, he thought. Harker was his immediate boss and they didn't really see eye to eye on anything. His eyes opened wide as he read the letter. He slowly shook his head in disgust.

It was true that he was expecting a replacement of Ahmed Ahaz, who had come to him as an inexperienced but qualified constable straight from Aykley Heads Police College in Durham some years ago. While working on Angel's team, Ahmed had passed the final into the CID, had recently been appointed sergeant, and immediately took up a position in the CID at nearby Rotherham. Angel admired young Ahmed. He reckoned that he had the making of a great detective. It was a great loss to Angel, and the Bromersley force but that was the way the system worked. His promotion could no longer be delayed. But Angel thought, this young lass, Cassie Jagger, female at that, could hardly have been sent to him to replace Ahmed, could she?

Angel stood up. He glanced at Cassandra Jagger. 'Sit down, Cadet,' he said. 'I won't be long.' Angel dashed out of the room with the letter and went up the corridor to Detective Superintendent Harker's office. It was the last office at the end. Angel knocked on the door and went in.

It was as sweaty as a kitchen in a curry house in Kolkata, but it didn't smell of spices, it smelled of menthol.

Harker, a skinny, bald man with the head like a turnip was at his untidy desk swamped in papers, ledgers, reports and medications.

He looked up. When he saw who it was, he wrinkled his nose, turned down the corners of his mouth and said, 'Oh it's you, Angel. What do you want?'

'There seems to have been a mistake, sir,' Angel said, holding up the letter.

Harker sniffed and frowned.

Angel said, 'A young girl has knocked on my door with this letter. It tells her to report to me, and it's signed by you.'

'There's no mistake?'

'What use have I for a young girl, sir? I mean . . . I'm running a homicide department not a hop scotch gala.'

'Since DS Ahaz moved on, I thought you said you needed a replacement?'

'I do, sir,' Angel said. 'But young girls are no replacement for Ahmed Ahaz. They can't speak coherently. They can't write intelligibly. They can't spell. They don't know any geography. They only know about "boy bands" and the bedroom habits of people they call celebrities.'

'That young woman is a qualified cadet, Angel. She's been through basic training and passed a medical. It's up to you to use her services, train her, direct her through to her promotion to PC then DC then, even Detective Sergeant if she's smart enough.'

Angel's eyes flashed. 'Yes, sir. But she is a *girl*, interested in boys and mobile phones.'

Harker breathed out noisily. 'Twenty-two percent of all police are women, Angel.'

'This isn't a woman. It's a girl.'

'And some of them make Commissioner. And she'll grow up. You've got to get used to women in the force, Angel.'

'Sir. I am *very* used to women in the force. One of my sergeants is a woman. But this Cassandra Jagger is a girl.'

'I've told you, Angel, she'll grow up. Now the decision has been made. If that's all you want, buzz off and get on with it.'

Angel stood up. His face was pained. He had to accept that he was stuck with the girl. He came out of the office and closed the door.

'I'll never get used to it,' he said as he stormed down the corridor and burst into his own office.

Cadet Cassie Jagger was sitting where he had left her. She glanced at his grim face and was alarmed. She stood up.

Angel went round to the back of his desk and sat down. He looked up at her and said, 'Well, Cadet Jagger, it seems that I am stuck with you. It might come as a shock to you, at your tender age, that I am your immediate boss. Any troubles, you always come to me first. All right?'

She nodded. 'Right, sir.'

'Now, long term, you have to learn how to catch murderers. Short term, I want you to watch and learn as much as you can, as quickly as you can. I want you to learn everybody's name, what they do, and where they are located. If they are witnesses, criminals or complainants, remember their names and all they say. Make notes if necessary. Make copious notes, if your memory isn't good. That's what you've got a notebook for. That's how you will earn promotion, pass your exams and be of the most use to the team in general and me in particular. Got it?'

'Got it, sir,' she said firmly.

He was pleasantly surprised at the answer.

'For the time being, maybe the rest of today and tomorrow, I want you to stay where you are and anything you don't understand, ask. Don't just sit there like a blancmange. All right?'

There was a knock at the door.

'Come in,' Angel called.

It was DS Trevor Crisp. He was one of the two sergeants on Angel's team. He glanced at Cassie Jagger and smiled. She returned the smile somewhat weakly.

Angel introduced them to each other then he turned back to Crisp and said, 'What have you got?'

'I don't think Frank Arrowsmith was his real name, sir. The info on the hospital admissions records is completely fictitious and leads nowhere. The address and phone number don't exist. Also his next of kin is bogus. During the nine days he was in hospital, he didn't have a single visitor or make a phone call.'

Angel nodded and rubbed his chin. 'Have you checked the phone book for any other Arrowsmiths?'

'No, sir. I could try that.'

Angel wrinkled his nose impatiently. 'Do it and let me know. Were any photographs taken of him by the doctor or the hospital *before* he had the operation? You know, either photographs for the surgeon to work from, or to record "before" and "after" pictures, for publicity purposes. These private hospitals like to do that.'

'I doubt it.'

Angel's face muscles tightened. 'Well, *find out*, lad!' he bawled. '*Find out*!'

Cadet Cassie Jagger was paying close attention to the discussion between the two men. She looked a little dismayed when Angel raised his voice to Crisp.

'I would have expected *you* to think of that,' Angel said to him. 'And let me know what you find out.' Angel rubbed his chin and added, 'And did he pay up front for anything?'

'I thought of *that*,' Crisp said, 'and he didn't.'

Angel nodded. 'No. Villains never do.'

'He owed the hospital several thousand.'

The phone rang. He reached out for it. 'Angel,' he said.

It was Harker again. 'Come back up here, straightaway,' he said.

'Right, sir,' Angel said and he replaced the phone.

He frowned and wrinkled his nose. The last place in the world he wanted to be at that time was back in Harker's sweat box.

He stood up, looked at Crisp and said, 'I'm going to see the super. Crack on with those inquiries.'

'Yeah, right,' he said and made for the door.

Angel looked back at the girl. 'Are you all right, Cadet Jagger?'

She smiled and said, 'Yes, sir.'

He pointed to the pile of papers, post and reports on his desk and said, 'There's this month's "Police Review" near the top of that pile. Familiarise yourself with it.'

'Oh. Right, sir. Thank you.'

‘I’ll have to find something for that lass to do,’ Angel muttered as he strode up the passageway to the superintendent’s office.

Angel reached Harker’s door at the same time as his opposite number in the uniformed branch of Bromersley force, Inspector Asquith.

‘Hello, Haydn. Have you had the summons as well then?’ Angel said.

‘Yes. What’s it about?’ Asquith said. ‘Do you know?’

‘No idea,’ Angel said.

They heard a loud coughing through the door. It had to be Superintendent Harker.

‘We’d better get in there,’ Angel said. ‘Won’t do to rattle his cage.’

Asquith smiled and knocked on the door.

‘Come in,’ Harker said, then followed it up with more coughing.

Angel followed Asquith in and saw Harker as usual behind his desk. Also, seated in a chair opposite him was another man, a stranger.

The man stood up and smiled at them. He was six foot three and as neat as a whisky straight.

Between the coughing, Harker made the introductions.

Angel and Asquith learned that the man was Detective Superintendent Ephraim Wannamaker of the International Antiques and Fine Art Unit, known as the IAFAU, which was linked to the Metropolitan Police and based in London.

They shook his hand.

Angel was pleased to note that he had a good, strong grip and that he held his hand for the accepted length of time with no affected display of strength or superiority.

‘Please sit down, gentlemen,’ Wannamaker said. Then he looked at Harker.

Harker held out an open hand to Wannamaker to indicate to him to carry on.

‘Well, gentlemen,’ he began, ‘I am here to enrol your assistance to catch a gang of thieves that Interpol are very concerned about. Let me tell you what *we* know. We have to go back to Germany in the thirties and forties. While the Nazis were in power, I suppose you will already know, they plundered cultural property from Germany and Austria and every territory they occupied. They stole art, antiques, and anything valuable, from Jewish families, from museums and private collectors and others.

'The treasures were stored in various hiding places throughout Europe, in secluded castles, tunnels, salt mines and caves. The mines and caves offered the appropriate humidity and temperature conditions for some artworks as well as protection from Allied bombing raids. It has been estimated that the number of objects hidden away was more than a million.

'Towards the end of the second World War, during all the confusion, crooks and collectors succeeded in raiding the hideouts and stealing huge quantities of these priceless works of art for themselves. Now, after 70 years, much of that illicit loot is being sold surreptitiously well below its true market value and turning up in this country.

'It should, of course, be returned to the families or museums from where it was dishonestly misappropriated from in the first place, if at all possible.

'Anyway an informant has told us that valuables are coming into South Yorkshire via the Republic of Ireland. Paintings and sculptures have been unloaded in the dead of night from a yacht at a lonely spot on the west coast of Ireland and then somehow smuggled across the Irish Sea to England.

'Now, gentlemen, have either of you recently in the course of your work come across any paintings, sculptures, or works of art of a very high standard? Possibly in the hands of villains or suspects?'

'No, sir,' Asquith said. 'Can't say that I have.'

Angel frowned. 'Nor have I, sir,' he said.

Wannamaker nodded. He seemed to have expected that response. 'Well if you do, please advise me or my department,' he said.

Angel said, 'Do you have any information about the gang or the gang leader or a description of him, or anything else to go on, sir?'

'No,' Wannamaker said. 'I regret that I haven't.'

'Well sir,' Angel said. 'I know you will want to keep secret the ID of the informants, but could you tell us anything at all about any of them?'

Wannamaker ran a finger up and down his temple. 'Erm, well,' he said. 'One of them was a man in Mountjoy Prison in Dublin. He said that he was paid two hundred pounds a night to transfer objects shrink-wrapped in black waterproof plastic, at the dead of night, from a motorised yacht to a cobble which was then rowed to an inlet on the west coast of the country and further loaded onto a lorry. You can rely on the information, Inspector. It has been investigated and confirmed.'

Harker sniffed and said, 'Well keep your eyes open.'

'And please report any findings or suspicions to me, Ephraim Wannamaker of the IAFAU. Here's my card,' he said, handing each of them a thick embossed business card. 'My phone number's on there. It's a direct line to my desk. Ring me anytime.'

'Right, sir,' Angel said.

* * *

Cow Lane, Tunistone, near Bromersley
Thursday, 10 March 2016, 11 a.m.

Mrs Buller-Price was returning home in her ten year old Volkswagen Passat from her weekly shop in Bromersley. She lived with her three dogs of assorted parentage and Tulip the cat, in an old farmhouse she rented halfway up a hill on the outskirts of the village of Tunistone, six miles from Bromersley. She was driving the car up the unmade road to the farmhouse, when she saw in the field on the corner a *Farmhouse To Rent* sign. It could only have applied to her home because there was no other property around there. Her nearest neighbour was half a mile away.

Her face went scarlet. 'Outrageous!' she grunted angrily. 'Absolutely outrageous!! We'll soon see about *this*.'

She stopped the car, got out, charged up to the sign and stared at it. It simply said that the farmhouse was to rent and interested parties should apply to the estate manager, Mr Lance Lidimont, c/o Walker and Wainwright, Estate Agents, 26-30 Victoria Street, Bromersley.

She leaned over the fence to try to reach the stake to pull it out of the ground and dislodge it. The sign was on a heavy stake that had been hammered into the turf. It was placed inside the field about a metre away from the wooden fence. Unfortunately, she was unable to reach it. She straightened up, red faced and panting, and stood in the lane her arms akimbo and glared at it. When she caught her second wind, she returned to the car, turned it round and made her way down the unmade road back to Bromersley.

Twenty minutes later, she arrived at the offices of Walker and Wainwright, the Estate Agents. She pushed open the glass door, eyed the young woman on the reception desk and waddled across to her with her large leather handbag in one hand and her umbrella with the duck's head handle in the other.

The young woman saw her coming and sensed trouble. She quickly swallowed, affected her best synthetic smile and said, 'Can I help you?'

Repressing her vituperation, Mrs Buller-Price gave her name and asked to see Mr Lidimont as civilly as she could manage. Several minutes later she was shown into his office. He came from behind his desk to meet her. He held out his hand to shake hers.

'Ah, Mrs Buller-Price,' he said. 'My name is Lance Lidimont, I am so very pleased to meet you at last. Do please sit down.'

The old lady was surprised at the reception which somewhat blunted the venom she had been planning to shower upon him. 'Thank you, Mr Lidimont,' she said. She put the big handbag on the floor by her side, and seeing no convenient place to stash her umbrella, retained it tightly in her hand. 'Perhaps you won't be so pleased to have met me, when you hear what I have to say.'

'Mrs Buller-Price, may I explain the situation to you?'

'Young man, the situation appears to be that you are attempting to boot me out of the house where I have lived most of my married life and since, without any warning and without any explanation. I have paid the rent in full and on the dot ever since my dear husband died, and he paid it and never missed before that. And I might point out that you have not kept up with the repairs, which is your part of the—'

'Do let me interrupt you there, Mrs Buller-Price, please.'

'Well,' she said, fixing him with a stare.

'If you look carefully at your lease, you will find under the heading of repairs and maintenance, that you and your dear husband before you, have always declined to vacate the property, even for a day, to allow tradesmen full and unfettered access. That is the reason why some of the necessary maintenance has not been done.'

The old lady pursed her lips. She knew that there was some truth in what he said. They had always declined to move out because they didn't want to move to a hotel even for a day or two and leave their personal and private possessions that had constituted a lifetime of happy memories behind, for workmen they didn't know to trample over.

Lidimont continued. 'Now the farmhouse needs re-wiring, re-pointing, some work needs doing on the roof and so on.'

She nodded in agreement. 'Well, how long would the workmen need, Mr Lidimont?'

'We don't know, but there is much more to it than that, Mrs Buller-Price. When all the repairs *are* done, including decorating inside and painting outside, the owners will need and be legally able to command a very much increased rent.'

Mrs Buller-Price's jaw dropped. Her several chins were accentuated by the lowering of her open mouth onto her chest. 'I don't think that I could afford a higher rent, Mr Lidimont.'

The estate agent smiled. 'Don't worry, Mrs Buller-Price. All is not lost. This morning, we have just received instructions regarding a property known as the Monks' Retreat, which has a location similar to the farmhouse. It has magnificent views of the Pennines. There are several acres of land with it, a stream and a small private lake within its boundaries.'

Mrs Buller-Price frowned. She was not at all sold on the idea of leaving the farmhouse which, for all its shortcomings, she had made very comfortable for herself and her pets, the last forty-five years.

'The Monks' Retreat sounds much bigger than the farmhouse,' she said.

'It is, but you don't have to use all the rooms, and the rent is exactly the same as the farmhouse, and it doesn't need any repairs or re-decoration. It's all ready for moving into.'

Her eyebrows shot up. The Monks' Retreat was beginning to sound a possibility and she relished the idea of a small private lake. She was thinking that she might be able to get out her waders and do a spot of fishing again. She hadn't been able to do that since her dear husband had died ten years ago.

'Now Mrs Buller-Price,' Lidimont said, 'I am authorised to allow a good tenant, such as yourself, two years rent free plus the cost of the actual removal.'

She blinked. It sounded too good an offer to refuse.

'I have the keys. Would you care to have a look at it?'

THREE

DI Angel's office, Bromersley Police Station, South Yorkshire
Thursday, 10 March 2016, 2 p.m.

There was a knock at the door.

'Come in,' Angel said.

It was Detective Sergeant Flora Carter, an attractive and highly competent police woman in her thirties. She had been at Bromersley force in Angel's team for almost two years. She saw Cadet Cassie Jagger sitting opposite the inspector and gave her a friendly nod.

The cadet returned a nervous smile.

Angel made the introductions and then to the cadet he said, 'You know what I have told you, make whatever notes you need.' Then he looked at the sergeant and said, said, 'Sit down, Flora. When we've finished here, show her round the station, the locker room, the canteen and so on, and fix her up with Ahmed's desk in CID.'

'Right, sir.'

'Now, tell me what you've got.'

Flora opened her notebook and said, 'I first spoke to Dr Saalheimer's secretary. She said she had not seen the man, but she knows there would have been some correspondence and notes from the doctor in a file with his name on, but when she went to it, it was empty. Arrowsmith must have cleared out the file before he left the hospital.'

Angel wrinkled his nose and rubbed his fingers hard over his mouth. 'I don't suppose it's any use asking how Arrowsmith arrived at the hospital. Did you find out if he came in by ambulance?'

'No sir, he didn't, sir. I checked on that. That's certain. Nobody else I asked had any idea how he came. It seems that he must have arrived under his own stream at reception with a suitcase. That's all I could find out about that. Then I spoke to the ward assistant who was on duty that day, Tracey Thorne. The young woman who kept the patients water jugs full and made the tea round. She hardly remembered who I meant. Then she said his head was always covered in bandages when she went into him. She used to fix him up with a glass straw in his cup so that he could drink it. Now she couldn't recall what he looked like after the bandages were removed.'

Angel stared closely at DS Carter. 'She saw him *after* he had had his bandages removed?'

'Yes, sir. But only briefly.'

His eyes narrowed. 'So she is the only living soul we know about who saw him with his new face.'

'Yes, sir.'

'Give me the hospital number?' he said as he reached out for the phone.

Angel soon reached the hospital manager's office and asked if it was possible to speak to Tracey Thorne.

The hospital manager said, 'I am afraid that Tracey Thorne isn't here. She should have reported for work at noon today but she has not yet arrived. It is not like her. She is most reliable.'

Angel raised his head. His eyes opened wide.

Angel's pulse went up twenty beats a minute. 'Is she on the phone?' he said.

'She's not on a land line,' he said. 'We've tried her mobile and it goes straight to voice mail.'

'What's her address?'

'I have it here. Hold on a moment, please . . . I have it. It's Flat 7, at Claremont House, Claremont Street, off Middleton Road, Bromersley.'

Angel banged down the phone, stood up, turned to Flora and the cadet and said, 'Tracey Thorne has not turned up for work. Come with me.'

They rushed out of the office to his car, a BMW, in the police car park at the rear of the station.

It took only a few minutes to reach the three storey stone mansion of days gone by. As the car slowed down, they glanced at the house door, then the windows and gutters and noticed that they hadn't seen paint for a good few years. The windows on the upper floors needed washing and one window had a pane of glass replaced with a piece of cardboard.

One concession to modernity was a nine-push-button box for verbal communication between tenant and caller attached to the stone arch surrounding the front door.

Angel looked down the names scrawled against each of the numbers. He noticed that number one was simply *The Concierge*, and number seven was *T. Thorne*. He thought how wise it was of her not to mention her gender in these uncertain times.

He quickly pressed Tracey Thorne's button and waited by the speaker grille. There was no reply. He pressed the button again, longer and harder. There was still no reply.

Angel and Flora exchanged glances. His eyes showed he was deep in thought and was not happy.

Flora said, 'She could be out shopping or . . . gone to her mother's.'

Angel said nothing.

Cadet Jagger frowned.

Angel pressed the concierge's button.

A gruff male voice said, 'Yes. What is it?'

'This is the police,' Angel said. 'I'm urgently trying to contact a Miss Tracey Thorne.'

'The police?' he said. 'Press button seven.'

'I have done. There is no reply.'

'Well . . . she'll be at work.'

'No, she isn't. There are urgent reasons why we need to check where she lives. The hospital gave us this address.'

There was a short pause. They could hear heavy breathing followed by a sigh. 'All right,' he said. 'I'll let you in. Close the door after you. Her flat's on the first floor. I'll meet you there.'

There was a click, a buzzing noise and the front door opened an inch.

Angel pushed it and it opened wider. Flora and the cadet went in. He followed them then closed the door firmly. They stepped forward a few steps over a layer of dried leaves left there by autumn winds and muddy boots, then through another door with glass panels of thistles and other flowers in deep purple and bottle green, leading to a hallway and a staircase. They mounted the uncarpeted wooden stairs noisily to the first floor then looked along the gloomy corridor until they found a room with a large seven painted on the door.

At that moment a big man in a brightly coloured checked shirt with a fleshy face and wet lips arrived jangling a bunch of keys. He looked them up and down and seeing Cadet Jagger in uniform was reassured they were the police.

His eyes eventually settled on Angel, being the most mature of the three. 'What's she been up to, then?' he said with a sardonic grin.

Angel turned away from him.

When the big man spoke, he had the sort of lips that resulted in spraying the one nearest to him with saliva.

The man peered at Angel and said, 'I know you.'

Angel looked at him. 'I'm afraid you have the advantage of me.

'You're that copper who *always* gets his man, like the Mounties, aren't you?' he said. 'I've seen you on the telly and in the papers often enough. This must be a murder case you're on?'

The muscles of Angel's face tightened briefly. People often said that to him. He was always worried that being honoured with that reputation it might jinx the very next murder case he was investigating. He said nothing. His only interest at that time was finding Tracey Thorne.

'Has the lass murdered a bank manager and run off with the money?' he said with a grin.

He didn't expect a reply because he immediately followed the quip with a hard bang on a panel on the door and said, 'Tracey. It's me, Jack Wing. If you're in there, open up. The police want to talk to you. *Tracey*!'

He waited a mini second and added, 'I've got the key. We're coming in.'

He pushed the key in the lock and opened the door.

Angel pushed his way forward. He saw a young woman fully dressed laid on the bed on her back motionless. His heart missed a beat.

'Wait here,' he said.

'What's happened?' the caretaker said, taking a step forward.

Angel glared at him. '*Stay back there*!' he said.

'Frigging hell,' the man said. 'What's happened?'

Angel approached the bed. He saw red daubs on her forehead. It was a name. It was 'Judas'. He knew he needn't check to see if she had a pulse, but he went through the motions. He put two fingers on her neck. She was stone cold. Her face was grey.

'Flora,' he said, without taking his eyes off the body. 'Ring SOCO. Tell DS Taylor to come out here ASAP. Then ring Dr Mac.'

DS Carter dug into her pocket for her mobile.

Cadet Cassie Jagger looked at the sergeant and said, 'Is she dead?'

Carter nodded as she concentrated on making the call.

The cadet gasped.

'Frigging hell,' the caretaker said and shook his head.

The cadet's face went whiter than the walls in Strangeways's loos. She stared trance-like at the young woman's legs hanging over the edge of the bed. Then quickly looked away.

Angel glanced round the room. It was an untidy mess, with clothes draped everywhere, and a side-table covered in bottles and pots of make-up. He squatted down and glanced under the bed. There were a few magazines and bits of underwear stuffed underneath. He was careful not to touch anything.

From that room were two doorways without doors. He glanced through both. One was a kitchen, the other a tiny shower and a washbasin. There was no sign of an intruder.

Angel came out of the room and closed the door.

* * *

DI Angel's office, Bromersley Police Station, South Yorkshire
Friday, 11 March 2016, 8.28 a.m.

The phone rang.

He reached out for it. 'Angel,' he said.

'Good morning, sir. Sergeant Clifton. The manager of Blackwood Quarries out at Deerspring has just been on the line. He has reported the theft overnight of a considerable amount of dynamite and fuse cord.'

Angel's eyes opened wide. 'A considerable amount? Just exactly how much?'

'One hundred and fifty sticks of dynamite and twenty-five metres of fuse cord, sir,' Clifton said.

'Wow!' Angel said. His stomach bounced up to his mouth and back. 'That's almost enough to blow Bromersley into the next world . . . Haven't they got an automatic intruder alarm link with the station?'

'Yes, sir. But there's nothing been reported in the incident book.'

'Did you say the manager reported it? What's his name.'

'Yes sir. His name is Herbert Lee.'

'Right, Bernie. Thank you. I'll see to it.' He replaced the phone but kept his hand on it. He was thinking about all the likely candidates there were who would have given their right arm to be in possession of that dynamite. There were the political nuts, declared enemies of the West, who would like to blow up a landmark building with all the people in it, villains who would like to break into a bank vault or even a prison, and sundry others. The list seemed endless. The number of possible crooks who could be responsible was far too extensive to be able to call on each one and try and suss them out.

Then Angel thought that if the robbery had been due to some man's carelessness at the quarry . . . how much delight it would give him to put a lighted stick up his backside.

A knock at the door interrupted his reflections.

It was DS Crisp. 'I checked the name Arrowsmith, sir, and there were two others in the phone book,' he said. 'I've visited them both. And they were related to each other. It was father and mother at one address and married son and daughter at the other. And none of them had even heard of our villain.'

Angel nodded and rubbed his chin.

Crisp continued. 'Then I checked at the hospital and there weren't any photographs taken of Arrowsmith either before or after the operation. I didn't think there would be.'

Angel looked up. His eyes flashed. 'I didn't think there would have been either. But we would have looked damned ridiculous if there *had* been photographs and we hadn't even bothered to *ask* for them, wouldn't we?'

Crisp gave a little shrug.

Angel's eyes grew even bigger. 'Well, *wouldn't we*?' he yelled.

Crisp was slow to reply. 'Erm, well, yes sir. I suppose so.'

The muscles round Angel's mouth tightened. He looked straight at Crisp and shook his head.

* * *

It was early that Friday afternoon when DS Taylor called on Angel in his office with a file of papers and a small polythene bag with the *EVIDENCE* printed in red on it.

'Sit down, Don,' Angel said. 'And tell me what you've got.'

'We've finished the crime scene, sir,' Taylor said. 'And I've brought Tracey Thorne's purse, sir,' Taylor said as he handed the EVIDENCE bag over. 'We couldn't find a handbag anywhere. Maybe she didn't have one.'

'I wouldn't know,' Angel said.

'There's not much to say, sir. We retrieved a lone dark brown hair and a few particles that could be human skin from her dress. We'll send that to the lab . . . might get DNA from them.'

Angel nodded. 'Anything else?'

'Not really, sir. Tracey Thorne's clothes and underwear in the flat were all bought from the cheapest shops, and most of it needed washing and ironing. But there were no drugs or signs of alcohol, no stolen goods, nothing illegal.'

'Any signs of a boyfriend?'

'No, sir. With all the powder and paint there was, I should think it wasn't because she didn't try.'

'Were there any prints in the place that weren't hers?'

'A few, sir, but none of them were made recently.'

'Any idea as to how access was made into the flat? Any damage to the door?'

'No. I reckon she must have trusted the caller and simply let him or her in.'

Angel shook his head, partly in disbelief and partly disapproval.

Then he told Taylor about the dynamite robbery and sent him out to the quarry manager's office to see what forensic he might uncover.

* * *

About an hour later, Angel phoned the mortuary to speak to Dr Mac.

'Now then, Michael,' Mac said. 'I suppose you want to ask me about the young lassie, Tracey Thorne.'

'Have you completed your examination,' Angel said.

'Aye. There's not much to say. A young healthy woman of about twenty-five, cause of death: asphyxiation. She had been choked. There are contusions on the throat corresponding with finger marks. Exactly like the murder of that nurse I did a PM on earlier this week.'

Angel nodded. 'We thought the murder was committed by the same man, Mac. Could you say that in court?'

'Aye. I'd put money on it.'

'Good. Have you got the time of death?'

'Aye. She'd been dead about thirty hours when I examined her in situ, which was three o'clock yesterday afternoon, so time of death would have been between seven am and eleven am Wednesday morning.'

'There's no evidence that they slept together is there?'

'No. Well, there's no evidence of any sexual activity recently. And she isn't pregnant. And she died where she was found and in that position on her back on top of the bed. She hadn't been moved.'

'Thank you, Mac,' Angel said.

'You're welcome. What's this Judas thing then?'

'I'm still working on it. I don't suppose the murderer is called Judas.'

'On each of the bodies, the word was written in capital letters, wasn't it? Perhaps the five letters are an abbreviation for something?'

Angel cocked his head slightly to one side. 'Could be,' he said. 'But *what*?'

'Just a suggestion, Michael. Just a suggestion. You'll no doubt solve the wee mystery in the course of time.'

Angel concluded the call and replaced the phone. He rubbed his chin. The post mortem hadn't really raised anything new. It had however confirmed, that the murderer *was* Arrowsmith. Tracey Thorne saw him *after* the operation and would have been able to identify him. There was only one thing to do and that was to plod on.

He reached out for the polythene evidence bag that Taylor had left with him. He opened it and shook out the purse. Inside it were forty pounds in notes, some coins, a mobile phone, two credit cards and a key.

He rubbed his chin, then reached out for his own phone and tapped in a number.

It took some time to be answered. Then a timid girl's voice said, 'CID. Cadet Jagger.'

'This is DI Angel. What's up, lass? Were you asleep?'

'No, sir,' she said.

'Well, what *are* you doing?'

'Nothing, sir.'

Angel reacted as if somebody had trodden on his toes. '*Nothing*?' he said. 'We can't have that. We'll have to put that right. Come into my office.'

The CID office was only across the corridor. It only took her a few seconds.

Cadet Cassie Jagger came in armed with her notebook and a pen. 'Yes, sir,' she said.

Angel looked across at her, picked up the mobile phone taken out of Tracey Thorne's purse and showed it to her. 'Do you know how to check out the calls made on a phone?'

Her eyes danced with delight. She was being given a job she knew.

'Yes, sir,' she said, and she took the phone out of his hand.

Angel was pleased at her eagerness and alacrity.

There was a knock at the door. 'Come in,' he said. It was DS Carter.

'Sit down a minute, Flora,' Angel said, then he turned back to the cadet. 'Right, carry on, Cadet Jagger. Let me have it ASAP?'

She smiled widely at him and dashed out.

He watched the door close, smiled and turned back to the sergeant. 'Right, Flora,' he said. 'What did you find out then?'

'Nothing useful, sir. I visited all eight flats and nobody saw or heard any strangers or visitors during the last week. Only two of the tenants knew her name was Tracey Thorne.

The caretaker chap, Jack Wing said that she seemed a lonely sort of girl, always on her own. He'd never seen her with anybody.'

Angel wrinkled his nose. That wasn't much help. He wasn't pleased. 'Right, Flora,' he said as he as he slipped the purse back into the evidence bag and sealed it.

'That her purse, sir?'

'Yes. There's money in it. It confirms that the murderer didn't kill her for her money, only because she would have been able to finger him.'

'Arrowsmith, sir?'

'I think so.'

'Another dead end then, sir?' she said.

'Not exactly,' he said. 'It makes me wonder if the murderer has some strange morality in his make-up.'

'You mean, he'll commit murder but not robbery?'

'Yes. Exactly,' he said. 'In which case, Arrowsmith or whoever he is, may be a homicidal maniac, who is likely to murder anybody he considers to be a threat.'

Flora's mouth dropped open.

Angel noticed. She looked afraid. He bit his bottom lip. He could have kicked himself. He shouldn't have been so outspoken.

'We've nothing to worry about,' he said. 'But we must be careful to conduct our interviews in pairs, that's all.'

Then he looked at his watch. It was half past three.

'Come on,' he said. 'A ride in the country will do us good.'

FOUR

It was thirty minutes later, when Angel accompanied by DS Carter were on their way in the BMW to Tunistone. This small market town was off the main road and down a country lane. It was a mile to the hamlet of Deerspring, to the Blackwood Quarries.

It was an impressive sight: a huge cliff about 180 metres high of white stone with massive bulldozers, lorries and other earth moving machinery working below. From that perspective, the machines looked like small toys crawling around at the bottom of the cliff.

As they got closer to the quarry, the country lane weaved round to the left to reveal a small two storey brick built building with a sign across the front that read: *Blackwood Quarries Ltd*. The windows were covered with iron bars built into the brickwork and there was a burglar alarm box fastened high up the front wall of the building. There were a dozen cars and a white van parked outside on a small area in front flattened to make a rough car park. Angel immediately recognized the van: it was SOC's Ford transit.

He drove straight towards the van and parked the BMW alongside it.

Just at that moment the door of the building opened and DS Taylor and two DCs came out. They were all carrying white canvas cases on shoulder straps. They began to cross the car park to their van. Taylor saw Angel and DS Carter in the car. He looked across and lifted a hand in to indicate that he had seen them. He gave the case he was carrying to one of the DCs and came straight across to the BMW.

Meanwhile Angel pulled on the handbrake and switched off the BMW engine.

As he advanced towards the car, Taylor was shaking his head. 'Good afternoon, sir,' he said. 'We're on our way back to the station. Apart from damage to the outside door of the building to gain access, there's no forensic evidence here. The scene has not been preserved.'

Angel's eyes flashed. 'What do you mean?' he said.

Taylor shrugged. 'The safe has had to be used. Apparently it was at Mr Lee, the manager's instructions.'

Angel's face muscles tightened. 'All right, Don. *I'll* see Mr Lee.'

'Do you want us to attend, sir?'

'No. You carry on.'

'Right, sir,' he said. He turned and made his way back to the SOC van.

Angel's looked at Flora and said, 'Come on, Flora. We'll go in and see this . . . Mr Lee. And I want you to take notes.'

Flora nodded.

They crossed the car park and reached the office building. Angel noticed the sturdy wooden door that had several recent and savage claw marks, presumably made by a crow bar, which had severely damaged the door and the door jamb.

Inside the building, they found themselves in a small entrance hall with three doors with names painted on them leading off it. In the background they could hear two men conversing. One of them sounded angry. It was unclear what they were saying. Reception was a small glass window with the word *Enquiries* painted neatly above it.

Angel peered through the glass. A middle-aged woman was working at a computer. Behind her he could see untidy piles of papers, books and envelopes on several tables, and against the wall an expanse of pigeon holes with more papers in each hole.

The woman saw him, looked up, lifted the little window, sniffed and said, 'Yes?'

'I want to see Mr Lee, please. Bromersley Police, DI Angel.'

'Oh, you've just missed the police,' she said. 'They've not been gone long.'

'No. I've seen *them*,' Angel said. 'It's the manager, a Mr Lee I want to see.'

She pulled a face. 'Well, he's a very busy man, I don't know if he'll see you.'

Angel's fists tightened so much that his fingernails pressed into his skin. 'I am Detective Inspector Angel of Bromersley Police. I am following up your report of a serious robbery overnight. If you don't tell him immediately that I am here, I will introduce myself.'

Her big eyes stared at him. Her jaw dropped open. She let go of the window. It dropped shut with a bang. She jumped up from the chair and disappeared out of Angel's vision.

Angel and Flora exchanged glances. She opened her shoulder bag and took out her notebook in readiness.

After a few seconds, they heard a man roar something unintelligible. Seconds later, the door closest to them was yanked open and a big man with a red and blue face, wearing freshly pressed dark navy blue trousers and bright red braces over a white and blue striped shirt dashed out in to the corridor. He was holding a pair of horn rimmed spectacles in one hand. He looked at Angel, then at Flora. He then glared back at Angel and said, 'I am Herbert Lee, manager of the quarry. Who is the big mouth who insists on seeing me?'

Angel stepped forward.

Flora looked at the two men. She bit her lower lip. Lee appeared to be three stone heavier than the policeman.

Angel wrinkled his nose. 'You must mean me, sir,' he said. 'I am here in response to your reported robbery.'

'That was last night, Corporal. Lots of things have happened since then.'

Angel took in a deep angry breath. 'I am an *Inspector* of police, sir. And I need to know why you did not protect the scene of the crime?'

'There was nothing to see. The thief or thieves broke into the place, came into my office, helped themselves to all the dynamite and fuse cord here and took off.'

'But our forensic team could perhaps have found evidence that is beyond the human eye to see.'

'There was *nothing*, I tell you.'

'You may be prosecuted for obstructing the police in the execution of their duty.'

Lee's jaw dropped open. He recovered quickly.

'Look here, Inspector,' he said, 'we had a robbery, I know, but life goes on, work goes on. This is a very busy quarry. On a good week we mine, wash, dry and deliver over a thousand tons of aggregates. That's a lot of muck and it's a lot of money.'

But Angel wasn't to be diverted. 'What happened to the alarm?' he said. 'It is connected by phone to Bromersley police station to automatically relay a pre-recorded message, but we have no record of any such call having taken place.'

'I know all that,' Lee said. 'It didn't go off for some reason. It wasn't ringing when I got here this morning.'

'Perhaps you didn't set it,' Angel said.

Lee's eye flashed. 'Of course I bloody *set* it. I set it *every* bloody night.'

'I'll be in touch with the alarm people, myself. I'll find out what exactly happened,' Angel said. 'These modern alarms have sophisticated systems that tell them when the alarm has not been set. Now I need to know where the dynamite and fuse cord were kept.'

'Why?' Lee said. 'They are not there *now*. Don't you understand? They were stolen. You should be out there looking for the thieves not bothering me with stupid questions.'

Angel stood his ground. 'I need to see where you stored the dynamite and fuse cord that you claim is missing?'

Lee ran his hand through his hair. 'Come in here,' he said. Then he turned and went back into his office.

There was a slim young man wearing spectacles sitting on a chair moving papers about on the desk. He pointedly avoided making eye contact with Lee as he entered. The big man tapped him hard on the shoulder from behind and said, 'Leave it for now. Get back to your office.'

The young man jumped up, jerkily gathered up some papers off the desk, then rushed past Angel and Flora out of the office as they came in.

The office had the usual fittings and furniture, plus a big black metal trunk next to a sturdy looking safe brick built into the corner of the office.

'You wanted to see where the stolen dynamite and fuse cord were stolen from?'

Angel nodded.

Lee pointed to the safe and then bawled, 'It was in *there*.'

Angel looked at the safe. It was a modern superior model. It had two keyholes, and there were red and blue wires under metal clips soldered around the lock across the front of the safe that disappeared down the side under the bricks and concrete and eventually to the alarm.

'Is it empty now?'

'There's some cash and some papers in there, that's all.'

'Will you open it up, sir?' he said.

Lee glared at him and said, 'What do you want it opening for? I've told you what's in there.'

Angel slowly breathed out a lungful of air. 'Will you open it up, sir, please?'

Lee pulled an ugly face. He reached under the kneel hole of his desk, picked up a briefcase, slammed it down on the top of his desk, opened it and took out two keys with shafts around 10" long. He then bent forward, inserted one key in one keyhole of the safe, and the other key into the other keyhole. He pushed them in most of the length of the shafts, turned the keys to a healthy clicking sound, then grabbed the handle and pulled open the door.

Angel leaned down and peered into the safe. He saw that there were three shelves. On the top shelf was a large red cash box. On the shelves below were three large ledgers and various brown envelopes held together with elastic bands.

Angel frowned and said, 'Is this where the stolen dynamite and fuse cord were taken from?'

'I said so, didn't I?'

'And are these books and papers and items usually kept in this safe?'

'Of course they are.'

'How much money is there in the cash box, sir?' Angel said.

'What's that got to do with the robbery?' Lee said. '*That* wasn't stolen. It is still here. I want you to find the robbers of the dynamite and fuse cord. This poking and prodding around is time-wasting nonsense. What have the contents of this cash box got to do with the robbery of the dynamite and fuse cord?'

Angel managed to keep his self-control. It wasn't easy. He breathed out noisily and said, 'How much money is there in the cash box, sir? An approximation would be fine.'

Lee ran his hand through his hair and said, 'I don't know. It's the petty cash. Between two and three hundred pounds, I suppose.'

'Is it locked?'

'No. It *isn't* locked. The key was misplaced years ago. Are you going to *check it*?'

'No, sir,' Angel said. 'Your estimation is good enough.'

'Thank you,' he said sarcastically.

Angel's eyes alighted on the big black metal chest next to the safe. He tapped it with his foot. 'What's in there?'

'There?' Lee said. 'Nothing.'

Angel frowned. He leaned down, opened the lid and looked inside. At the bottom of the chest were several sticks of dynamite. He counted them.

'Nothing?' he said. 'You call six sticks of dynamite nothing? They should be in the safe.'

'First thing this morning, when I found that we had been robbed of all our explosive, I phoned our quarry in Stockton and got them to send a driver with ten sticks so that our operations wouldn't be halted and the men put out of work. Our shot firer took four sticks, that's why there are six left in there.'

'That's not the point, sir,' Angel said. 'The dynamite should be kept in that safe and not in this tin box. And it looks as if you have regularly kept it in there instead of the safe.'

Lee ran a hand through his hair again. 'Those few sticks have only been here about an hour,' he said. 'Of course we keep it in the safe.'

'You wouldn't be able to get 150 sticks in that safe, and the safe certainly hasn't been forcibly opened. If the safe had been robbed, the thieves would almost certainly have taken the petty cash as well. I have reason to believe that you have broken several crucial conditions of your licence to store explosives, also, you have hindered the police in the execution of their duty.'

Lee opened his mouth to say something, changed his mind, shrugged and sat down at his chair behind the desk rubbing a hand across his mouth.

'Don't you realise that even one stick in a villain's hands could be very dangerous indeed?' Angel said. 'And by the way, you should put the six sticks you have in your safe immediately.'

Lee looked up at him briefly then looked away.

'In addition,' Angel said, 'you have contaminated the scene of the crime — if indeed there was a crime — so much so that it makes it highly improbable that we will be able to catch the thieves.' He then shook his head and said, 'You will be hearing from us very soon. Good day.'

* * *

It was seven o'clock on Tuesday evening, 15 March.

Mrs Buller-Price had accepted the generous deal offered to her by Mr Lidimont of Walker and Wainwright and had moved from the farmhouse to the Monks' Retreat the previous day.

The transition had been much easier than she had expected. Everything went without a hitch. However, she was very tired and so she spent a quiet evening having only a roast beef sandwich she had prepared the night before, and a pot of tea for her evening meal, before settling the dogs and the cat down, and going upstairs to bed at the unusually early hour for her of eight o'clock.

She had also been very busy the following day, Tuesday, getting everything where she wanted it and trying to understand the push button controls on the central heating which was entirely new to her.

Her three dogs had taken to the change of residence after they had sniffed and followed trails that led nowhere around the grounds and the inside of the house. They found places on the Axminster to lie down close by her as soon as they saw that she had settled. Tulip the cat had not taken to the new house so easily and jumped from one piece of furniture to another ostensibly trying to find the highest accessible point in the room.

At seven o clock, that Tuesday evening, Mrs Buller-Price poured herself a wine glass of Campions Ginger Wine — one of her favourite tipples — which she had found in the course of packing up for the move. She then flopped into an armchair, that she had strategically placed to enable her to look through the downstairs sitting-room French window across the lake. The sky was cloudless so that the moonlight shone on the water. She could see as far as the bushes at the far side of the lake. The table lamp at her side annoyingly reflected on the panes of glass in the windows. She reached out, switched it off and it markedly improved the visibility of the view outside. Sitting in the dark induced a sort of naive magic looking across the water through the trees and bushes illuminated only by the moon.

She poured herself another glass of the wine and sipped it gently. As she sat there, she relaxed and smiled broadly: she was congratulating herself on being fortunate enough to be established in the big house with a lake, many trees and bushes along the perimeter of it, a small rowing boat in the boathouse and acres of land with enclosed ample traffic-free land for the dogs, all rent free for a year!

She looked out at the lake and yearned for the day when she had the time, and the weather was a little warmer, so that she could put on her waders, if they still fitted, and take her rod into the lake and fish as she had done several years ago. She had found that it was so soothing and restful for her mind and her soul.

Moments later, she yawned, as she wondered what sort of lives the monks had led when they occupied the house many years ago. She was mulling it over when she thought she saw some activity at the boathouse. Her pulse began to beat like a drum. She swallowed. She sat forward and peered through the window. Seconds later, and the double doors of the boathouse opened and the small rowing boat sailed out.

She gripped the arms of the chair so tight that her knuckles turned white.

There appeared to be two men in the boat. They were wearing big coats with cowls. Then she realised . . . of course . . . *they must be monks*!

She saw the boat glide across the water to the farthest point and then out of sight. She peered intently for some time towards the point at which they had apparently vanished, but saw no other activity.

The next thing she remembered was being startled by Schwarzenegger, her Great Dane, planting a heavy paw on her knee and making noises that she knew meant he was bored staying inside and he wanted to go out.

She switched on the table lamp and peered at her watch. Her jaw dropped onto her chins when she saw that it was 1.30, the early hours of Wednesday morning. She must have been asleep in the chair four hours or more.

* * *

It was 8.28 a.m. later on the same morning of Wednesday, March 16 when Angel went into his office at the station. He took off his coat and hat, hung them on the hook on the side of the stationery cupboard, sat down at the desk and reached out to pull the pile of paperwork nearer to him. The phone rang.

It was Superintendent Harker coughing and wheezing on the line. 'Is that you Angel?' he said. 'Just had a triple nine . . . A woman . . . she says that she has found two bodies . . . her sister *and* her niece . . . in a house . . .'

Angel's heart began to pound again. It was hard to keep up with all the murder cases being discovered on his patch at that time.

'What's the name and address, sir?' he said.

'The woman's name is Eloise Collins,' Harker said. 'The address where she found the bodies is 21 Park Road. And Angel, you need to be aware that she was *very* distressed.'

'Right, sir,' Angel said.

'Get on with it then,' Harker said and then he replaced the phone.

Angel set the wheels in motion. In addition to his usual investigative team, he enrolled WPC Leisha Baverstock to act as liaison officer. She had been on a special police course and had some experience of what was needed. She would take Eloise Collins away from the scene of the crime, look after her, seek medical help if she considered it necessary, and gently obtain as much information regarding the two deceased and any other persons she knew of who might be involved in their murder as witnesses or suspects.

When all his team were on the job, Angel sat back in the chair considered the situation. The two reported deaths were the fourth and fifth in 9 days. It was a very worrying time.

* * *

Mrs Buller-Price slept soundly and awoke at seven o'clock in response to the alarm clock on that Wednesday morning. She quickly completed her ablutions, dressed, breakfasted and by nine o'clock she was ready for anything. She went into the hall, pulled out her umbrella with the duck's head handle from the hallstand and opened the front door. Her three dogs rushed out. She stood on the front doorstep and the dogs stood round her to see which direction she was going to take. She locked the door, put the key in her pocket then turned to survey the lake and trees in the sunshine. She wished that her dear husband, Edgar, had still been alive. He would have enjoyed living in the Monks' Retreat and he would already have been in that boat in the middle of the little lake, with his rod over the side, fishing.

After taking in a few big breaths, she marched towards the lake. The dogs followed. She stopped at the boat house. A rather primitive, small, shed-like building on a raised wooden platform that projected about five metres into the lake. She lifted the sneck of the door and opened it. The dogs wanted to be inside the place. They rushed past her and in their enthusiasm, the black Labrador was pushed off the wood-walk into the water.

Mrs Buller-Price watched her, smiled and said, 'Come out of there, Zsa Zsa.'

The dog ignored her, she was enjoying the water. She swam along the side of the boat towards the other end of the boathouse then disappeared under the exit door.

Mrs Buller-Price wasn't a bit afraid for the dog. She knew Zsa Zsa was very much at home in water. She was a strong swimmer. The dog would have surfaced easily in the lake at the other side of the door. Nevertheless, she shook her head, annoyed at the dog's disobedience.

She looked around the little boathouse. She was there to see if the boat was where it should be and had not been disturbed. The two oars were on the floor of the little boat, it was tied properly to the post, the doors at each end of the boat house were closed and latched. Everything certainly looked in order.

It seemed to confirm that what she thought she saw the previous night, was in reality a dream, and that she didn't really see monks or anybody else sailing in the boat.

She held the door open and looked down at her other two dogs. 'Everybody out,' she said. 'Come along.'

The two dogs obediently followed her out of the boathouse onto dry ground. She closed the door and dropped the sneck.

She began walking round the edge of the lake, towards the trees and bushes. The dogs raced ahead barking with excitement. Then a metre or two in front of her she saw the Labrador, Zsa Zsa arriving at the edge of the lake. The dog looked at the old lady as she struggled to get a grip on the bank to pull herself out of the water but couldn't get a good enough foothold.

Mrs Buller-Price wrinkled her nose. 'I told you to come out in the boathouse, Zsa Zsa,' she said. 'Now you see you're stuck. I'm not going to help you. I shall get filthy wet, and I am wearing my very best new blouse.' She gestured with a hand and said, 'Try further down.'

The dog turned away, slithered back into the water and swam off.

Mrs Buller-Price walked on for a few minutes on a thick soft carpet of amber, red, brown and black coloured leaves through the trees and bushes, keeping as near to the lakeside as she could, enjoying the quiet beauty of the bright sun shining through the bare tree branches sprouting new buds and the bushes, mostly evergreen. Then a black, wet Labrador rushed up to her, wagging her tail and looking very pleased with herself.

Mrs Buller-Price was glad to see her, but she said, 'Now don't come fussing round me, Zsa Zsa, making me all wet and muddy.' She waved her arm and pointed ahead and said, 'Go find the others.'

Zsa Zsa barked then dashed off, wagging her tail.

Another few minutes and Mrs Buller-Price reached the position on the bank which was about the farthest point from the house . . . the place where she thought the boat went out of sight.

About a metre from the lakeside, the dogs were circling, sniffing and inspecting the leaves. At one point, Zsa Zsa was pawing the leaves, as if she wanted to uncover something.

Mrs Buller-Price watched her.

Schwarzenegger joined in the rummaging around about. After a while, the two dogs got bored, left the spot and Zsa Zsa put her nose down close to the ground and made a bee-line through some trees to a high stone wall, which was the boundary wall of the monastery. The dog looked up the wall and barked several times. Schwarzenegger appeared from out of the bushes and he and Zsa Zsa dashed off together.

Then Mrs Buller-Price's smallest, ugliest and most disobedient mongrel dog, Bogart came across to where the two big dogs had been pawing the leaves. He sniffed and began with the tiniest of paws, to imitate them.

Meanwhile Mrs Buller-Price looked around. There were no signs of any recent human activity anywhere. It confirmed that what she thought she saw was a dream, and she was glad of it. She really could not have strangers — even if they *were* monks — doing whatever they were doing so close to the house. She shuddered. She hoped she wasn't going dippy in her old age. She remembered her mother telling her about her old aunt Martha who lived to be ninety-nine. She was reputed to have seen people who had died, and had conversations with them. But that was a long time ago.

She considered whether to turn back or continue round the lake on the other side. She decided to press forward as she hadn't yet seen the other side of the lake. She had only taken a few steps when Bogart arrived. He wanted to attract her attention. He stood in front of her bouncing like a ball, his tail wagging like helicopter blades, preventing her moving forward. He was obviously excited, but for some reason wasn't barking. The other two dogs ran up to see what was happening.

Mrs Buller-Price stopped leaned forward and said, 'What is it Bogart?' It didn't take her long to realise why he wasn't barking. She spotted something small sticking out of his mouth. 'What have you found?' It was gold coloured. She held out an open hand. 'Give it to me then,' she said.

He brushed the palm of her hand with it, and then pulled back.

‘Oh, you want me to play?’ she said, then shook her head. ‘Come along, Bogart. Give it to me.’

She held out her hand again. The dog darted forward touched her hand with his nose then ran back a little way. ‘Oh dear,’ she said. ‘Bogart, are you going to give it to me or not?’

The dog reset it between his teeth and showed her a bit more of the gold coloured item.

She smiled. ‘You’re teasing me, aren’t you?’

She put her umbrella over one arm, leaned down, picked Bogart up. He wasn’t pleased. He was surprised, he struggled and protested, repeatedly digging his back feet into her chest.

Mrs Buller-Price’s eyes flashed. ‘You’ve dirtied my new blouse, Bogart.’

She took hold of the gold coloured item sticking out between the little mongrel’s teeth. The dog released his grip and she took it from him. ‘Thank you, Bogart,’ she said. ‘Thank you very much indeed.’

She lowered him to the ground.

The gold coloured thing he had brought her was a panel about 3 cm x 2 cm. It didn’t weigh much so she knew it wasn’t gold. She thought it was a sort of plaster, painted or gilded. It seemed old. Engraved on the panel were the four capital letters INRI. On the reverse side was an area in the middle of the surface that looked like dried glue, the sort of stuff that was made from the hooves of cattle and horses years ago. There were superficial scratches caused by the dog’s teeth, but otherwise Bogart had not damaged the find. She wondered if it had been outside, open to the elements since the days of the monastery. It wasn’t dirty. Perhaps the odd shower of rain and the concealing with dried leaves had helped preserve it. It made her wonder again about what she thought she had seen the previous night.

FIVE

It was 1.30 p.m. There was a knock at Angel's office door. 'Come in,' he called.

It was Police Cadet Cassie Jagger. She had two sheets of A4 in her hand.

He looked up. 'Yes, lass, what is it?'

She licked her lips and peered at him nervously. 'I've checked off the calls on Tracey Thorne's mobile phone over the past month, sir. Did you want me to go back any further?'

Angel's face brightened. 'It's not taken you long,' he said. 'No. That's far enough for starters.'

She sighed with relief then smiled. 'Right, sir,' she said as she handed the details over to him.

He took them, glanced at them and then put them on top of the pile of papers in front of him. 'If we find that we have need to prove a long-standing relationship with a particular person, or anything like that, then we might have to go back further.' He rubbed his chin. 'Who did she make the most calls to?' he said.

'Ninety per cent were to her friend, sir, another young woman, Sybil Roberts, who does the same job in the hospital on the trolleys as she did, delivering teas and so on. The other calls were to shops or businesses selling things. There wasn't any family or anybody else. I was able to verify every call.'

He nodded and smiled. 'Right, Cadet,' he said. 'By the way, I can't call you Cassandra. It's too long. It would waste time. What does your mother call you?'

'Cassie, sir,' she said. Unless she's mad with me. Then I get Cassandra.'

Angel nodded. 'Right, Cassie. Now, I've a very important job for you. Go to Elmdale Hospital. Seek out Tracey Thorne's friend on the trolley, this er, Sybil Roberts, and ask her if Tracey ever told her anything about the man we know as Frank Arrowsmith. Anything at all. The smallest detail could be vital.'

The brightness of her eyes showed how eager she was to do the job. 'Right, sir.'

'Go to the Control Room and smile at the duty sergeant. Tell him I told you to try to cadge a lift there.'

Her eyebrows shot up. She grinned. 'Yes, sir.'

The phone rang. He glanced at it then looked back at the young cadet.

'Go on then. Off you go. And *don't be long*.'

Cadet Jagger was off like a rocket. The door closed.

He reached out for the phone. 'Angel,' he said.

It was a young PC on reception. 'Sorry to bother you, but there's a peculiar old woman in reception. She wants to see you. She says she knows you. She's says her name is Buller-Bright or something. Shall I tell her you're busy, sir?'

Angel's face muscles tightened. 'No. You will not. Her name is *Mrs* Buller-Price, I believe. She is a very polite, gentle and correct old lady. You will treat her with the utmost courtesy and politeness. And you will *show* her down here to my office *straightaway*.'

The young PC's face reddened. 'Yes, sir,' he said smartly.

Angel had not seen or heard from dear Mrs Buller-Price for several years. She had always been a most fervent charity worker, advocate of animal rights and general supporter of good works. She was as honest and straight-forward as anyone Angel knew. And he was very fond of the old lady. She reminded him of his favourite grandmother.

A few moments later, she was seated in Angel's office with the point of her umbrella on the floor and both hands on the duck's handle. She told him about her change of address, the reason why, and the matters leading up to her bearing the small, gold painted plaster panel with the letters INRI engraved on it. She also told him briefly about her dream.

Angel looked at it and said, 'It looks old, Mrs Buller-Price but I'm no expert. It's rather like a plaster called gesso, which is what the beautiful frames around pictures and paintings are moulded from. I don't know what the word INRI means, although I know I have seen it somewhere.' He swivelled round to the table behind him and picked up the old dictionary and began to turn the pages.

Mrs Buller-Price said, 'Well, my dear Inspector, what really troubles me is this. Do you think that this little panel was accidentally left by the monks *before* they left sixty years ago, or was the dream I thought I'd had, not a dream at all and the monks really have returned?'

'Mmm. I don't really know, Mrs Buller-Price,' he said without looking up. His nose was in the dictionary. Then he suddenly said, 'INRI. It's *here*. The letters are an abbreviation of the Latin, *Iesus Nazarenus Rex Iudaeorum*. Translated that's "Jesus of Nazareth, King of the Jews." It's the inscription placed over Christ's head during the Crucifixion.'

Her mouth dropped open. 'Oh yes,' she said. 'I also thought I'd seen it somewhere. Well, Inspector, it looks as if the monks could have left it all those years back. Must have fallen off a crucifix or similar.'

Angel nodded and smiled. 'Something like that.'

Mrs Buller-Price says, 'Well thank you, Inspector. You've certainly put my mind at rest. If I had thought of it, I could have looked it up. I must go. I know how busy you are.' She stood up.

'There's no reason to rush away. I'll get somebody—'

'You're very kind, but I know you are run off your feet, besides I must get back home to my dogs, and I want to call at Beddowes for a sack of mixed wild bird seed before he closes. I have to look after a whole new family of birds at the Monks' Retreat, you know.'

Angel smiled. 'Wait a moment, my dear lady. I'll get someone to see you out.'

Angel picked up the phone and asked for reception.

Angel and Mrs Buller-Price made their cordial goodbyes, Angel assuring her that she was always welcome if she was in trouble and Mrs Buller-Price apologising for disturbing him and promising to bring him a homemade gooseberry fool the next time she came to see him. Then the young PC who had showed her to Angel's office was now given the job of seeing the old lady safely off the premises and to her car.

Angel looked up at the clock. It was almost 5 o'clock. Unusually he hadn't heard from SOCO who were still working at 21 Park Road, the location of the double murder.

He reached out for the phone and tapped in a number.

DS Taylor answered.

'What's happening, Don?' Angel said. 'How are you progressing? Found anything interesting?'

'Nothing that you would call interesting, sir,' Taylor said. 'We are packing up for the night now, but should be through by nine or so in the morning. There are two separate scenes to cover, so it's taking us that bit longer.'

'Right, Don, goodbye.'

He replaced the phone.

* * *

The following morning, Thursday, Angel was in his office as usual at 8.28 a.m. He was scanning through the post to see if there was anything important that couldn't wait to be attended to, when there was a knock on his door.

'Come in,' he said. It was Cassie Jagger.

'Good morning, sir,' she said brightly. 'I managed to speak to Sybil Roberts, the workmate of Tracey Thorne at Elmdale Hospital. She does the same job, with the drinking water and the teas and so on, that Tracey Thorne did, but over on the other side of the hospital. She did confide in her to some extent. She said that she, Tracey, had said that she didn't like Mr Arrowsmith. He was rude and bossy. She said that he expected her to knock on the door and that she should say who she was before she came into the ward.'

'Hmmm,' Angel said. 'Anything else?'

'Sybil Roberts said that Tracey Thorne never saw his face, because his head was totally covered in bandages including his eyes. He also must have damaged his hand. She said he had one finger bandaged. That's all.'

Angel's forehead creased. He rubbed his chin. 'A finger bandaged? That's interesting,' he said. 'This Sybil Roberts . . . could she say which finger and which hand?'

Cassie's face dropped. 'Sorry, sir. Sybil couldn't remember whether Tracey had said or not. That was all she *could* remember.'

'It's not much to go on.'

'She wouldn't have remembered *that* much, sir,' she said, 'if it hadn't been for Nurse Riley and the man arguing about it. The nurse had said it was no longer necessary for the bandage to be on. And she started to take it off. But he made a big fuss and angrily insisted that he wanted it left on. So it *was* left on.'

'That might be useful, Cassie,' he said. 'Sometimes these details become significant. We now know that the murderer has a finger that had needed bandaging for some reason recently.'

Cassie Jagger beamed.

He put the morning's post on top of the existing accumulation of papers and pushed them to the middle of the desk top.

Then he stood up. 'Come on, Cassie,' he said. 'We're going to 21 Park Road.'

He leaped up from the desk, reached out for his coat and hat and made for the door.

Cassie Jagger's eyes narrowed. 'That's the crime scene isn't it, sir?' she said as she followed him out of the door. 'I don't know if I'm ready for *that*, sir?'

He sighed. 'I'm *never* ready for it. It's the job.'

* * *

Angel and the cadet soon arrived at 21 Park Road. It was a semi-detached house built in the thirties. There was a uniformed PC on the doorstep and the usual assembly of police vehicles parked in the street.

Angel rang the doorbell. It was answered by a member of the SOCO team who was dressed in the customary sterile white suits, caps and masks.

DS Taylor came across to them.

'I was about to ring you, sir,' he said. 'We've just finished the scene. Both bodies are still here. We'll be ready for the search after they've been removed.'

Angel sniffed. 'You've been long enough.'

Taylor pulled a disagreeable face. 'There are *two* bodies and *two* crime scenes, sir.'

'Well I'm here now, Don. By the way, this is Cadet Jagger.'

Taylor and Cassie exchanged smiles and nods.

'Tell me, Don, have these two bodies got "JUDAS" daubed on their foreheads?'

Taylor said, 'Yes, sir. And it looks like the same red lipstick used on the other bodies.'

Angel ran his hand through his hair. He bit his lip and then said, 'Right,' he said. 'That's five murders this man has committed.'

He rubbed his chin hard.

He turned to Cassie and said, 'Make a note of anything you see and hear to do with these two murders. All right?'

'Right, sir,' she said.

'Very well, Don, what have you got?' Angel said.

Taylor said, 'A woman about thirty was found dead on the settee in the front room. We believe her name is Sarah Steadman. We think that she lived here with her widowed mother, aged about fifty-five. We believe the mother's name to be Cora Steadman. She was found dead on the floor in the kitchen. There seems to have been something of a tussle between the murderer and Cora Steadman. Some of the ornaments on the sideboard and the occasional table against the wall in that room have been knocked over. We have found several loose hairs on both bodies, also some fragments of skin from under the fingernails of Cora Steadman from which I expect to be able to get DNA.'

Angel nodded. 'Good. Are there any signs of a forced entrance?'

'No, sir,' Taylor said. 'They must have known him.'

'Not necessarily,' Angel said, rubbing his chin. 'He had a brand new face.'

Taylor nodded, 'Of course.'

Angel rubbed his chin. 'Anything else? Fingerprints? Footprints?'

'No, sir. That's about it.'

'Is Dr Mac here?'

'He's at the back, in the kitchen. Still working on Cora Steadman.'

'Right Don, let's see the body in the front room first then . . . that's the daughter, Sarah Steadman isn't it?'

'Yes, sir. Through here,' he said.

Angel followed him two paces down the hall to the door. Then he stopped and turned. He noticed Cassie Jagger hanging back. She saw him. He reached out to her. She bit her bottom lip as he gently took her by the arm and steered her through the door ahead of him.

They were in the small, comfortable-looking sitting room with a 58 inch TV screen in the corner. A settee was in the middle of the room. The head and most of the body of Sarah Steadman lay along the seat; the hips were bent, the knees over an arm and the feet hanging loose. The staring open eyes looked towards the ceiling. She was dressed in casual clothes, a yellow jumper and denim trousers. One of the shoes she had been wearing had slipped off and was on the floor.

Angel was looking for the cause of death. There was no blood. He spotted bruising round the dead woman's throat. He saw the red lipsticks marks on her forehead spelling out the word "JUDAS". It was exactly like the others.

Cassie was trying not to look at the body but as Angel stared at the dead woman's face, Cassie glanced at it, then became quite bold and had a longer look. A cold shiver ran down her spine. It seemed to her that it was like looking at somebody still alive but frozen in time.

Angel turned to Taylor. 'Everything exactly as it was found, Don?'

'Dr Mac had to move the body, sir, for his examination of her, but it was put back as near possible as it was found.'

Angel nodded.

Then he heard Dr Mac's Glaswegian twang. He was speaking to somebody in the hall. 'Did I hear the Inspector arrive?' he said.

'I'm in here . . . the front room, Mac,' Angel called out.

The doctor pushed the open door further and came in. He was still in the obligatory white suit. 'There you are, Michael,' he said. 'I am aboot finished here. I want to have the bodies moved to the mortuary.'

'Right, Mac. Let me first ask you about this one.'

'Aye, well, I'll do my best.'

'What was the cause of death?'

'Asphyxiation, Michael. You can see contusions made by the murderer's fingers on the trachea.'

Angel nodded. 'I've seen them.' He sniffed and said, 'Anything else?'

'Let you know after the PM.'

Angel sighed. 'In your examination here, did you find anything unusual?'

'No. Nothing. You know I would have told you if I had.'

'Have you the time of death?'

'Er yes,' Mac said. He looked at his watch. 'Between 18 and 22 hours ago.'

Angel frowned then said, 'About seven o'clock last night?'

'Aye, give or take.'

'Thank you, Mac,' he said. 'By the way, are you short of two fifty pence pieces?'

Mac looked at him with a puckered brow. 'What are you on aboot, Michael?'

'In the old days, it used to be a couple of pennies, but they shrunk in 1971, when we went decimal. Now it takes two 50 pence pieces to keep their eyes closed.'

'Oh *that*?' Mac said. 'I'll get her eyes closed soon enough when I have her on the table.'

'I should hope so,' Angel said, then he turned to Taylor. 'Where's the other body?'

'The mother, Cora Steadman, sir,' Taylor said and he directed them out of the sitting room, past the bottom of the stairs and another door. 'She's in the kitchen.' They followed him down the hall. He pushed open the kitchen door.

They saw the figure of woman sitting on the red tiled kitchen floor leaning against the back door. She also had the word *JUDAS* in red lipstick on her forehead.

Angel went into the room followed by Cassie and Mac.

Cassie flinched at the grotesque sight of the body of the older woman with the red marks on her forehead.

Angel said, 'Have you got the cause of death, Mac?'

'Aye. It's the same. Asphyxiation, and again, you can see contusions made by the murderer's fingers.'

Angel crouched down and peered at the neck of the body.

'Can ye see them, Michael?' the doctor said.

'Pity they're not fingerprints,' Angel said. 'Have you the time of death?'

'Aye. It's the same time. About seven o'clock yesterday evening.'

'Thanks, Mac.'

Angel stood up. He looked round the tiny room. It was a kitchen like any other kitchen. It was clean and very ordinary. He turned round and went back into the hall.

'I'll just have a look at the rest of the house. Come on, Cassie.'

The doctor sniffed. 'Afore you go, Michael. Do you want to see any more either of the two corpses?'

'No,' Angel said. 'They're all yours, Mac. Thank you.'

Mac waved an acknowledgement, took out his mobile and began to make a call.

Angel opened the other closed door leading from the hall, and he and Cassie went through it into the other downstairs room. It was the dining room and it was clean, but in a mess. There were two dining chairs on their sides, cushions on the carpet, and glass ornaments broken on the floor. It had obviously been the scene of a scuffle, and Angel assumed it would have been between the murderer and Cora Steadman.

He took it all in then suddenly he turned to Cassie and said, 'Have you seen the ladies' handbags anywhere?'

'No, sir. Shall I ask Sergeant Taylor?'

He nodded and she went into the hall. He heard her muttering to Taylor and his response. A moment later they both returned.

Taylor walked up to a chair by the fireplace and said, 'I saw a bag, which I assume is Cora Steadman's down here, sir.'

He reached down to the floor and with one finger picked up by one of the straps a conventional leather handbag with a gilt frame and passed it to Angel. 'That's one,' he said. 'I think that is probably Cora's. Her prints were all over it.'

'Thank you, Don,' Angel said. He could see the aluminium dusting powder on the highly polished leather. He moved over to the dining-room table with it.

Taylor said, 'It might be that Sarah Steadman didn't have a conventional handbag, sir. There is a red sort of plastic purse on the settee where she was found. We haven't opened either of them yet.'

Angel said, 'Right, Don. Thank you.'

'Leave you to it, sir,' Taylor said and he went out.

Angel turned to the cadet and said, 'Fetch me that purse, will you, Cassie?'

Then he quickly went through the contents of Cora Steadman's bag. He seemed to be looking for something quite specific. He went through all the pockets, then through the wallet. He wasn't interested in the money. He put everything back and closed the handbag.

He stood looking at the wall in front of him, still with a hand on the bag. He was thinking. He obviously hadn't found what he was looking for.

Cassie appeared with the plastic purse.

Angel quickly opened it and poured the contents on the table. It contained money, a credit card, a mobile phone and a lipstick. He looked at the lipstick carefully. He wanted to make certain that it wasn't 'Passion Pink' made by Honeymoon. It wasn't. He picked up the mobile phone and gave it to Cassie and said, 'You know what to do with that, don't you?'

'Yes, sir. You want to find out who she called over the past two weeks?'

'Make it four weeks. And check on this landline here, also.'

Then he quickly stuffed the rest of the contents back in the purse and gave it to Cassie. 'Put that back where it was,' he said.

Cassie nodded. She could tell that he was put out by something. 'Right, sir. Have you found what you were looking for?'

'No. I was expecting to have found a photograph of Philip Marx or Frank Arrowsmith or whatever he is currently calling himself. But there aren't any being carried by either of those women. Of course, since then he has had a complete change of face so it is probably irrelevant. I just wanted an idea. Something tangible. We are looking for an illusion, a figment of poor Dr Saalheimer's imagination. Nobody can identify him. Nobody knows what he looks like or what his name is. This is an impossible job.'

Cassie didn't know what to say. She waited. Then he said, 'Get me Don Taylor.'

A few moments later Cassie Jagger and Don Taylor came into the room.

Ah, Don,' he said. 'When you are searching this place, if you come across any photographs, put them together. I want to see them.'

'Right, sir,' he said.

'Thank you,' Angel said.

Taylor went out.

Then Angel turned to Cassie and said, 'Make a note of this scene, anything out of place, broken and so on.'

'I have done, sir.'

He blinked with surprise. 'Right. Let's go upstairs.'

There were three rooms and a bathroom upstairs. They were spotlessly clean, well ordered and nothing out of the ordinary.

As Angel and Cassie came downstairs Mac and Taylor were talking. Dr Mac had discarded his white togs and was holding his big black bag. As Angel approached them the doctor broke away from Don Taylor.

'Don't run off yet, Mac,' Angel said.

The doctor smiled. 'You know I canna leave before ma meat wagon arrives. What can I do for you?'

Angel rubbed his chin. 'Well, which one was murdered first?' he said.

Mac said, 'No idea.'

Taylor said, 'We think it was the young one, sir. We think that Sarah Steadman was in the house by herself, that the murderer either knocked on the door or it was unlocked and he let himself in. He murdered her in the front room. Then her mother Cora arrived and saw what had happened to Sarah and tried to get away from him. But he attacked her, probably in the dining room, which would explain the damage and untidiness. She tried to avoid him but he chased her round the downstairs rooms. Eventually he caught up with her at the back door . . . as she was trying to get out of the house.'

Angel's jaw muscles tightened. 'Mmm. Makes sense. She must have been terrified. Poor woman,' he said.

SIX

Later that morning, Angel and Cadet Jagger returned to the station in Angel's car. There had been little conversation during the short journey. The sight of the two dead bodies had affected both of them. It had subdued Cassie Jagger and spurred Angel on to find the killer before he struck again.

As they walked down the corridor of the station, Angel said, 'Type up your notes and let me have a copy ASAP, Cassie.'

'Right, sir,' she said as she turned off into the CID office.

Angel's office door was opposite. He went in and before taking off his coat and hat he picked up the phone, scrolled down the numbers and clicked on one.

A young woman's voice said, 'DC Baverstock.'

'Leisha, it's DI Angel. How are you getting along with Mrs Collins?'

'Oh, she's a lot better than yesterday, sir. I am with her now in her own home.'

'Is she all right to leave for a short while?'

'Oh yes, sir. For an hour or so, I should think.'

'Right,' he said. 'I want you to return to the station and tell me what you've got.'

'Right, sir. I'll be ten minutes or so.'

He ended the call, but as he put the phone back on its cradle, it rang out. He put it back to his ear.

It was Flora Carter. She was ringing in to say that she had finished the door to door and had nothing useful to report. Nobody knew the Steadmans very well and nobody had seen or heard anything helpful at the critical time. DS Crisp phoned shortly after that and reported the same.

Needless to say, their news didn't help to lift Angel's mood.

* * *

It was 11.15 a.m. — exercise time for the forty prisoners on the top landing of D wing at HMP Poulton, near Sheffield.

For thirty minutes, most days, the inmates were allowed into the exercise yard which was a ten-metre-high walled area about a quarter the size of a football pitch. The only breach in the metre-thick wall was a narrow gate or door made of steel bars that led to the main prison building. Overhead, extending across the entire area of the yard, was spread heavy duty wire netting welded to rivets that passed through the walls near the top.

Some of the prisoners were walking round the yard in ones or twos or more. Several were leaning against the wall with their hands in their pockets and a skinny hand-rolled cigarette in their mouths.

The three prison officers supervising the men were at the prison side of the steel gate which they had locked. They were gazing through it, chatting about nothing of consequence, when they heard the roar of a very loud machine alarmingly close by. For a moment, they couldn't identify what it was. Then they were amazed to see a helicopter above them lowering three men dressed in black. The men descended from the machine like spiders onto the middle of the steel netting over the yard.

One of the officers immediately sounded the alarm, and bells and sirens made an almighty racket all round the prison and its environs.

A few prisoners rushed to the yard gate which of course was locked. They shook it and said, 'Let us in. Let us in. Let's get back to our cells. We are being attacked!'

The prison officers ignored them. They had their own troubles. They gazed upwards through the barred windows.

The men in black had long handled wire cutters and were rapidly cutting out a small hole in the middle of the wire netting cover. Several prisoners stood immediately under the hole in the netting and looked upwards at them, smiling and yelling enthusiastic encouragement.

Seven or eight other prison officers arrived including the prison governor. They looked upwards through the barred window and saw what was happening. The governor said, 'Unlock the gate. Let's get in there.'

The senior prison officer on duty at that point quickly inserted the key in the yard gate to unlock it.

However, the prisoners who had been crying out earlier to be let out of the yard had surreptitiously, in the confusion, threaded two plaited lengths of rope about four metres long through the bars on the gate. The rope had been stolen from the mailbag shop over a period of time. Both lengths were plaited into three strands for strength and each of the four ends was in the hands of a hand-picked, heavy prisoner supported by several others.

The prison officers could not open the steel gate. They strained to pull it but it didn't budge. They would never open it as long as the four prisoners kept a tight hold on the ends of the ropes. Given time, of course, they could cut or burn the ropes, but time they had not got.

'Let us in!' the prison governor screamed. 'You'll be up for report! It'll put six months on your sentences!'

The racket the helicopter made, combined with the bells and sirens, was deafening. To add to the frustration of the prison officers, they saw that a loop on a hook from the helicopter had been lowered through the hole in the netting, and one of the prisoners, a big man, had stepped into the loop, positioned it under his buttocks, looked up, waved and the helicopter rapidly winched him up through the hole to freedom and with the three men in black still suspended it flew away.

When the helicopter was out of sight, the four heavies on the yard gate released their grip on the ropes and joined the other prisoners amid wild congratulatory cheers. Many of the prisoners, danced around the square, some took off their shirts waved them in the air to simulate flags or bunting. Inside the prison there was the clanging of tin mugs against iron bars tapping out the letter V from the Morse code.

* * *

It was twelve noon. And Angel was in his office with PC Leisha Baverstock.

'Well, Leisha, did Eloise Collins tell you of anybody who had a grudge against her sister or her niece?'

'No sir. Not a grudge,' she said consulting her notebook. 'But she said that her niece, Sarah Steadman, had been in a depression for the last four years because of something that happened to the man she was engaged to.'

Angel frowned. 'What sort of something? Do you mean a row?'

'No, sir,' Leisha said. 'It was much more serious than that. Sarah had been severely depressed ever since the attack on the man she was going to marry. Eloise Collins said there was no consoling her. She was forever at the doctor's and the hospital. She had course after course of anti-depressant pills. She said, her mother couldn't do anything with her.'

Angel frowned. 'Attack? What sort of an attack?'

'He was mugged in the street, and left unconscious in the snow. He went into a coma.'

Angel's fists tightened. 'That's outrageous. Was this in Bromersley?'

'Yes, sir. Close to where he worked.'

Angel rubbed his chin. He thought he could possibly remember that case, 'What was his name?'

'Philip Marx, sir,' she said.

'That's an unusual name, Leisha. Four years back. Mmmm, I should have been able to remember that,' he said then he frowned and pursed his lips. At last he said, 'No, I don't recall it.'

'He was pounced on in the street by several men. It was behind Moore & Moore, the advertising agents in that old converted hotel on Inkerman Street in Old Town. He was a copywriter there.'

'He worked there?'

'Yes, sir.'

'And she was in that state because of this attack on him?'

'Yes, sir.'

'And were the attackers found and charged?'

'I don't know,' she said. 'I didn't think you'd want to go back that far.'

Angel rubbed his chin. She was right, but he smarted at the injustice of what had happened.

'What happened to him?'

'Her aunt didn't know. She thought he had died.'

Then he said, 'What did Eloise Collins make of the women having the word Judas on their foreheads?'

'She thought it horrific, but she made no other comment.'

'Is there anything in what she said that would link the deaths of her sister and her niece to the deaths of Dr Saalheimer, Nurse Riley and Tracey Thorne and a man who called himself Frank Arrowsmith?'

'No, sir. It is a complete mystery to her.'

His facial muscles tightened. 'She's not the only one.'

The phone rang. He reached out for it. 'Angel,' he said.

It was DS Clifton, the duty sergeant in the station control office. 'I thought you'd like to know, sir, that there's been a jailbreak from Poulton. There's all hell let loose in Sheffield and Chesterfield. Mick MacBride is back out. He'd only served five months of an eight year sentence.'

Angel's face dropped. MacBride was one of the big time robbers and racketeers that Angel had put away. Now, after only five months he was free again.

Clifton gave him all the details of how the escape had been managed.

Angel sighed. He ran his hand through his hair and wondered if anybody was ever going to bring him any good news.

He replaced the phone and turned to Leisha. 'Where were we? Yes. I know. Did Eloise Collins tell you anything at all about the past of either of them that could be seen as a grudge or a reason for somebody, a man, to want to kill them?'

'No. Not at all, sir.'

The phone rang again. Angel glared at it then said, 'Excuse me, Leisha.'

He reached out for it. 'Angel,' he said.

It was Dr Mac.

'Ah, Michael,' he said. 'In the course of my examination of the elder of the two females, Cora Steadman, I have discovered that she has a fractured skull due to a heavy blow to the head.'

'Thanks, Mac. Is it likely that it would have stunned her?'

'Most certainly. The weapon was either very heavy or it was delivered with a super human amount of force.'

'Mmmm. That would confirm what we were thinking, wouldn't it?'

'That the murderer *had* to kill Cora Steadman because she had caught him in the house?'

'Yes,' Angel said, rubbing his chin. Then he said, 'What about the lipstick? Is it the same lipstick used on all five bodies?'

'Looks like it. I have not done any comparison tests there yet, Michael. I'll check it out and let you know.'

'Thanks, Mac,' he said. 'There's something else. Do you remember examining a corpse by the name Philip Marx, sometime after Christmas Eve 2012?'

'It would be much easier if you gave me the exact date of his death.'

'I haven't got that, Mac.'

'Hold on, Michael. I'll tap his name into the er . . . . . .'

Angel heard the clicking of computer keys.

As second later the doctor said, 'Are you there, Michael? I'm afraid I have no record of the corpse of Philip Marx ever been examined by me. That covers the period from 2002 to the present day. Of course, if his death was from natural causes, I wouldn't have been involved.'

'Or *thought* to be from natural causes,' Angel said.

'Well, aye. There is always that possibility, Michael,' Mac said. 'Are you sure he died in the borough? I wouldn't be consulted if he died out of the borough, you know.'

'I don't know anything, Mac. Just fishing.'

He thanked the doctor and returned the phone to its cradle.

'Right, Leisha. Now I want you to go the office of the Registrar of Births, Deaths and Marriages and find out the actually date and location of the death of Philip Marx.'

'Right, sir,' she said. Then she smiled, put her notebook away and went out.

Angel rubbed his chin. This case wasn't coming together at all. Who and where was the missing man Philip Marx? Why should he or anybody else want to conceal his death?

He picked up the phone and tapped in a single digit.

A bright, young, female voice answered. 'CID. Cadet Jagger. Can I help you?'

'Come over here, Cassie. I have a little job for you.'

A minute later Cadet Cassie Jagger was seated opposite him, her eyes bright and fixed on him.

'Go to the town hall,' he said. 'Find the office where the electoral roll is kept. Show them your ID. They should have realised from your uniform that you were in the force, but make sure they understand the inquiry is a police matter or they might want to give you a bill. Find out what you can about Philip Marx from the electoral roll. If he can't be found on the current one, he should come up on last year's roll or the one before that. If you still get no joy, ask them to check out his existence on the 2011 census.'

'Right, sir.'

* * *

It was nine a.m. on Friday morning that Mrs Buller-Price was enjoying her third slice of toast and marmalade and her second cup of Darjeeling in the sitting room of the Monks' Retreat and avidly reading *The Times*, when she saw something that stopped the chewing and compelled her to put her teacup back in its saucer.

'Oh, Schwarzenegger,' she said to the big Great Dane. 'Listen to this. On the front page. It's about poor Mr MacBride.'

Schwarzenegger and the other three dogs gathered round her as she pulled back from the breakfast table at the Monks' Retreat, in front of the big window that overlooked the lake.

She folded the newspaper to a convenient size, held it up and angled it to receive the best light. She began reading it aloud then slipped into silence as she became more absorbed in what it said.

'Look, there's a photograph of him. It isn't a good one. He looks *very* glum. Of course being in prison won't be any fun. Look at what the headline says, *MacBride escapes from Poulton jail.* Then it goes onto say,

'*Mick MacBride — member of the gang that carried out that daring robbery of the Northern Bank in Manchester in the 1990s and other robbery offences — has escaped from Poulton Prison.*

'*MacBride, 53, was winched upward from the exercise yard at 11.30 BST today by helicopter.*

'*All ports and airports have been alerted.*

'*Detective Superintendent Horace Harker who is in charge of the investigation into the escape, said that the incident was well organised and "executed with clockwork precision." He also said that "there was no doubt that the escape had been successful because of collusion from inside the prison." He also said, "There is no suggestion that any prison officer has been involved."*

'*Police say that it was a commercial helicopter stolen earlier that day from Leeds. It was later found abandoned in a school playground in Tuniston.*

'*An operations room has been set up and the area cordoned off. People living near the prison are being interviewed by the police.*

Superintendent Harker has warned the public not to approach MacBride as he may be armed and dangerous.'

* * *

Mrs Buller-Price lowered the paper, looked at the dogs and said, 'What do think to *that*? Poor Mr MacBride. Armed and dangerous, it says,' she said. 'Huh. Armed and dangerous. How ridiculous. Mr MacBride armed and dangerous. They don't know him like we do, do they? He's a pussy-cat.'

Tulip, the cat meowed in agreement down from the picture rail.

Mrs Buller-Price looked up, smiled, and said, 'I'm glad you agree, Tulip.'

Then she looked down at Schwarzenegger, Zsa Zsa and Bogart. 'Of course, he shouldn't have robbed those banks like he did,' she said. 'But I expect he was one of the poor. He simply couldn't afford to keep his wife and children . . . I wonder if he has a wife and children? I must ask him that next time I see him. Oh, but I won't be able to see him. He won't be in Poulton Prison to see, will he? And he's not likely to be walking down the High Street with all the police looking for him either. Oh dear. Poor Mr MacBride.'

* * *

The phone rang. He reached out for it. 'Angel,' he said.

It was Detective Superintendent Harker. 'Come up here,' he said. 'I need to see you straightaway.' Then the phone went dead.

Angel's nose went up and the corners of his mouth went down. He went out of his office, closed the office door, and trudged up to the top of the corridor. He knocked on Harker's office door and went in.

'Sit down, Angel,' the superintendent said. 'As you may be aware, the responsibility for investigating this prison break has fallen on my shoulders.'

Angel dreaded the next part of what he was going to say.

'So I will be looking to you to deal with it as quickly as possible. I want you to find out who instigated the plan, who—'

'Excuse me, sir,' Angel said. 'Have you forgotten that I am in the middle of searching for a serial murderer. A man who has murdered five people to date. I need to catch him before he murders anybody else.'

Harker sniffed and said, 'I am fully aware of that, but you can easily run this investigation in tandem with the murder inquiries.'

Angel knew he'd say something ridiculous like that.

'There are *five* victims, sir. Most of them have entirely different backgrounds and murdered in three different locations, and I have this case to deal with as well as that dynamite robbery out Tunistone way. I have to prepare the charge, interview the witnesses for CPS to bring it to court, and so forth.'

'I know all about it. But *that's* not urgent.'

Angel gasped. 'Catching and booking a serial murderer is not urgent?' he said. 'And there's the matter of the stolen works of art that are supposed to be coming to crooks in this part of the world.'

'You have two detective sergeants you can delegate those non-forensic inquiries to them.'

Angel ran his hand through his hair and said, 'Can I make a suggestion, sir?'

Harker's eyes flashed. 'No, you *can't*,' he said. 'I need you to start *today*.'

'Why don't you take *one* of my sergeants for your inquiries, sir. I can't easily spare Crisp, but if it will get you off the hook, I will—'

Harker's eyes flashed. His thin blue lips tightened. 'I'm not on any hook, Angel,' he said. 'You talk like Hans Christian Anderson, you really do. If you can step out of that fantasy world you live in for a few minutes and remember the executive directly in charge of this station, you will probably remember that it is the Detective Superintendent, which is me. All right?'

Angel sighed.

'So listen up,' Harker added.

Angel had no choice but to listen to the briefing. But at the end of it he was absolutely clueless as to where Mick MacBride might be. He could be in Bromersley, but equally, he knew he could also be on the Costa Del Sol or in Rio De Janeiro. It was surely MI5's job to deal with prison breaks.

In addition, Angel knew that although the family of the four prisoners who hung onto the rope threaded through the gate to hold the prison officers at bay during MacBride's escape would have been exceedingly well rewarded, and that would also ensure than none of them would mutter even one helpful word to the police.

Angel came out of Harker's office angry and worried. He could not possibly take on board the search for MacBride together with his current case load. The cases had absolutely no concurrent features. By the time he had reached his own office, he had made a decision. He sent for DS Crisp.

'Ah, Trevor,' Angel said. 'Come in. Sit down. Regarding Mick MacBride's escape from Poulton, I want you to find him. I want you to start at the prison. There's bound to be some coverage by CCTV there. Look at that. See if you can identify anybody. Speak to the men who assisted the escape, also their families. Then see what you can find out about the helicopter. There aren't that many choppers about the place, nor chopper pilots. Then there's the three men who cut through the wire netting. They are likely to be local. Check that at the probation office. Then look at recent releases. Also look at his known associates immediately before sentencing for his last crime. Search their houses. They might be sheltering him. See what you can dig up.'

Crisp frowned. 'It's a tall order. What about MI5? Aren't they making the investigation? It's their pigeon, isn't it?'

Angel held out his open hands palm upwards. 'I don't know about them. The order has come down from on high.'

Then he looked at Crisp knowingly, and said, 'You *know* how it is, lad.'

'Will I be getting any help, sir?'

Crisp blew out a long breath and looked down at the floor.

Angel screwed up his eyes. He was loathe to make any concession. 'Well, take Ted Scrivens,' he said. 'He's coming along very well.'

Crisp looked up. 'Right, sir,' he said and made for the door.

Angel watched the door close. He sighed. His facial muscles tightened briefly. He regretted giving him the services of Ted Scrivens. It was one pair of hands less for his own inquiries.

SEVEN

Angel reckoned that the next most important fact he needed to know was to identify the weapon used to stun and fracture Cora Steadman's skull. It might be totally inconsequential, but equally, it might have a relevant bearing on the case.

So he left the office, got in the BMW and drove up to 21 Park Road again, the home of Mrs Cora Steadman and Sarah, her daughter.

There was a uniformed PC on the front doorstep. But no other sign of life.

Angel went straight to the kitchen where her body had been found.

He visualised what had probably happened. He thought that the murderer had been in the front room having killed Sarah Steadman, when her mother came in the house unexpectedly by the back door. She probably called out. Something like . . . 'It's me, Sarah. Where are you?' The murderer would have heard Cora's call. He would have had to make a decision. He must either get out of the house without being seen by her, or, if that was not possible, he must make sure Cora didn't see him to be able to identify him later. And the only certain way was to kill her.

Meanwhile, Cora curious as to why she had had no reply from her daughter, would call out for her again and begin to look round the house for her.

The murderer might still have been uncertain what he must do. He might have found somewhere to hide in the room. Angel looked round. Perhaps behind the curtains. He checked them. The lower part of the legs of his trousers and his shoes would have been visible. It was no good. There was nowhere else to hide in that small room.

Cora came into the room, found Sarah's body and was immediately shocked and emotionally devastated. Then Cora saw the murderer, and, at that horrific moment, ran out blindly out of that room into the room next door, the dining room. The murderer followed and a race began dodging round the table, eventually she ran into the hall and into the kitchen to the back door. She desperately tried to get out of the house away from him. But he caught up with her at the back door. She fought like a tiger, countering his moves as best she could. Then Angel noticed next to the sink, a gas oven. It had a corner about waist height. If the murderer caught Cora Steadman's head between his hands and banged it down on the corner of that steel cooker, it could crack her skull, weaken her considerably enabling him to finish the job by choking her as he had done with Nurse Riley, Tracey Thorne and Sarah, her daughter.

Angel was satisfied that that was something like the pattern of events that led up to the way Cora Steadman had been murdered.

He returned to the station to find PC Baverstock outside his office door. 'Ah, Leisha, come in,' he said. 'Have you had any luck at the Registrar's then?'

She followed him into the office and said, 'No, sir.'

He raised his eyebrows, his pulse rate quickened. 'No?'

'Nothing known,' she said. 'There is no record of the death of a Philip Marx. I checked the book from 24 December 2012 to the present date.'

Angel's face tightened. He pressed his lips into a fine line.

'All right, Leisha,' he said. 'Thank you.'

She went out.

Angel sat down and breathed out a lungful of air. He scratched his head. The name of Philip Marx kept cropping up during these investigations but nobody seemed to know much about him. Suddenly he jumped up, grabbed his coat and hat, bounced out of the office, up the corridor and outside to the car. He was determined to find out about the man. He was going to call at the place where the man Marx had worked. They should know something about him. He stopped the BMW outside the front door of Moore & Moore, the advertising agency.

He showed his ID to the receptionist and said, 'Can I see the person in charge please?'

'Could you tell me what it is in connection with?'

'It's a confidential police matter,' he said. 'And very urgent.'

Her eyes and her mouth opened wide. 'Oh. Oh I see,' she said. 'Oh. Please take a seat.'

Angel sighed and reluctantly slumped into a comfortable armchair, one of four that surrounded a rectangular coffee table with a vase of daffodils and several old copies of *Advertising Weekly* and *Campaign* on it. The reception area of an advertising agency seemed an incongruous setting in the old building which would have been at one time the saloon bar of the public house when it was built 200 years ago.

He had hardly taken in the surroundings when the young lady leaned over her counter and said, 'Mr Moore will see you now, sir.'

Angel was pleased he not had long to wait. He quickly rose to his feet and followed her through the nearest door into an office.

Introductions were soon over and Angel was seated opposite a gentleman of mature years asking him his first question. 'What can you tell me about a man called Philip Marx. I understand he used to work here.'

Moore's face creased as he looked downwards. 'Yes, he did. A personable young man. A good worker. Creative copywriter. Got along with everybody. He was here for about six years. That's a long time in this business. He might have been creative director now if it hadn't been for the brutal attack four years or so ago that put him in a coma. That was the end of him. A dreadful way to go for such a likeable chap with such a promising future.'

'Did you see him in hospital?'

'I didn't I'm afraid, but some of the staff did. I know that Nigel Hobbs in the creative department saw him because I remember him telling me that he was not conscious and there was no hope.'

'May I see him?'

'Yes, of course,' he said as he reached for the phone. He muttered something into it then replaced it in its cradle. 'He's coming down.'

'Thank you,' Angel said. 'Were there any others?'

'I'm sure there were. Nigel was quite close to Philip Marx. He'll be able to tell you.'

Angel nodded. 'Could you tell me Philip Marx's last known address?'

'I have it here,' Moore said. He pulled open a drawer in his desk, took out a book, placed it on his desk, opened it at the letter M, turned over a couple of pages then said, 'Flat 14, Montpelier House, Fountain Street. That was the last address we had for him.'

Angel scribbled it on the used envelope he kept in his inside pocket.

There was a knock at the door. It was Nigel Hobbs, a happy looking young man about thirty. He had long hair, an earring in one ear, wearing jeans and a red jersey.

Angel thought that he was either trying to grow a beard or he was in need of a shave.

Hobbs looked at Angel then at Moore. He put on his best smile, raised his eyebrows and said, 'You wanted me, Mr Moore?'

'Ah, Nigel,' Moore said. 'Sit down a minute. This is Inspector Angel. He's looking into the death of Philip Marx. You knew him pretty well, didn't you?'

Hobbs' smile deserted him. 'Oh. Oh,' he said. 'Well, erm . . . yes, Mr Moore.'

Then he turned and looked at Angel. 'I suppose I knew him Inspector, as well as anybody here. We worked together. We are, were both copywriters.'

Angel said, 'And did you visit him after he had been assaulted?'

Hobbs' lips tightened. His eyes narrowed. 'Erm, yes, I saw him a few times.'

Angel sensed that he was a reluctant witness. 'Tell me about it.'

Hobbs sighed. 'It's . . . it's four years ago now, you know.'

'Well, tell me what you remember,' Angel said.

Hobbs thought a few moments then said, 'Well, the first I heard that anything was wrong was when I came back to work here after Christmas and Phil didn't turn up. It was the buzz all round the building that there'd been a disturbance in one of the back streets, on that Christmas Eve, shortly after he had left us, and that Phil had been badly beaten up and was in the general hospital. I phoned through to see how he was, and it wasn't good news. That evening I visited him and was shocked to see him in a side ward, unconscious, his face mangled up, tubes in his mouth and up his nose, and other wires and machinery and equipment round him. It upset me, I don't mind telling you. I went a couple more times, but it was just the same. There was no change in his condition. The best information I could get was that he was in a coma and very seriously ill.'

Angel nodded. 'So what did you do then?'

'Nothing, really. I suppose I should have kept visiting him, but it was pointless. We couldn't have a conversation or anything. I couldn't take anything or do anything for him. I asked the ward sister how he was, and she gave me the official line that there was "no change", but I pressed her further and she said that when and if he came out of the coma, because of the injuries to his head, there was no telling how it might have affected his brain. He could be all right, but it was by no means certain. Visiting him just upset me to no purpose, so I stopped going.'

Angel rubbed his chin. 'And what happened to him then?'

Suddenly, Hobbs' eyes flashed angrily. His wriggled his shoulders uncomfortably and said, 'How should I know? I wasn't his keeper. I wasn't even related to him. I couldn't keep going to the hospital and seeing him like that. It was a complete waste of time.'

Angel looked at Hobbs' unhappy face. Angel noticed that Moore also looked pained.

Hobbs became aware of them closely observing him. He jumped up, turned away and said, 'Now, if you don't mind, Inspector, I've told you all I know. I can't tell you anything else. I am going to return to my desk. I've a lot of work to do.'

Angel rubbed his forehead and looked down. 'Yes, all right, Mr Hobbs,' he said. 'And thank you for that. Before you go, could you tell me who else visited Philip Marx while he was in hospital and was — shall we say — close to him?'

Hobbs frowned, then said, 'Yes . . . well there was Tom Skerritt for one. He's manager of the creative department. I remember that. Then there's Teresa Scott, she's an artist. And, er—'

At that point, Hobbs' face creased. He rubbed his chin. 'You know, Inspector,' he said. 'I think pretty well all six or seven in the creative department here at the time visited Philip in hospital, some time or another. But at least three of the team have since left and been replaced.'

Moore said, 'I can find out exactly who they were from the salaries book, Inspector.'

Angel turned to him. 'Thank you, sir.'

Hobbs looked at his employer, 'You don't want me for anything else, Mr Moore, do you?'

Moore shook his head. 'Not if the Inspector has finished with you.'

They looked at Angel. 'Thank you, Mr Hobbs. That's fine for now.'

Hobbs nodded and went out.

Moore looked wryly at Angel and said, 'I don't envy you your job, Inspector.'

Angel smiled. 'It has its compensations . . . sometimes,' he said.

He rubbed his chin. His unfocused eyes moved very slightly to the left and then to the right and then back again. It wasn't the first time a witness had turned indignant to delay further questioning. He was determined to watch Hobbs very carefully. He thanked Mr Moore, took his leave and returned to his office at the station.

* * *

It was about eleven o'clock when Angel came through the office door, he was followed in by Cadet Jagger.

'What is it, Cassie,' he said as he took off his coat and hat.

'I want to report on my visit to the town hall about Philip Marx, sir,' she said.

'Oh yes,' Angel said. 'Sit down. What have you got,' he said as he took his seat behind the desk.

'It wasn't difficult, sir. Philip Marx was on the electoral roll all right from 2011, all the way up to 2014. But he was *not* on the electoral roll in 2015 and 2016? So he either moved out of the borough or he is dead.'

'Or he didn't fill the forms in for those years because he wanted to disappear.'

'Yes, sir. That's what it looks like.'

'Mmm,' Angel said. He rubbed his chin. 'Were there any other people living in the flat with him?'

'No, sir. According to the roll he was living there on his own.'

Angel wasn't pleased. He didn't seem to be able to get any really hard news about what had happened to the man.

'Well, thank you, Cassie. Carry on,' he said.

'Right, sir,' she said. She stood up but was reluctant to go. She slowly made for the door, hoping Angel would call her back to give her another investigating job, but he didn't, so she left.

Angel leaned back in the chair and looked at the ceiling. He rubbed his chin. He took out his envelope from his inside pocket and looked at Marx's old address, Flat 14, Montpelier House, Fountain Street. He must send somebody round there or go himself. He was considering which to do when the phone rang. He reached out for it.

It was Doctor Mac. 'There you are, Michael. I have a bit of information for you. It *might* help your inquiries along.'

Angel was guardedly optimistic. 'I'm all ears, Mac,' he said. 'What is it?'

'The red daubs of *Judas* found on the five bodies I have here is from the same lipstick made by the Honeymoon brand of make-up. From their colour chart it is called "Passion Pink".'

Angel smiled. That could turn out to be a very valuable clue. It was also clear indication that the murders were committed by the same person.

'That's great, Mac,' he said. Angel suddenly had the feeling that he should be doing something physical such as chasing after a car, fighting a villain or arresting somebody, but there was nobody in his sights.

'Thank you *very* much, Mac,' he said.

'Anytime,' Mac said. 'We aim to please. Toodle pip.'

Angel grinned and replaced the phone.

His eyes narrowed. He wondered in what other way that specialised piece of information might be used to assist the inquiry.

He leaned back in the chair and half closed his eyes. He reached up to an earlobe and massaged it between his finger and thumb for a minute or so. Then he leaned forward and picked up the phone. He tapped in a single digit. It was soon answered.

'CID. Cadet Jagger. Can I help you?'

'This is DI Angel,' he said. 'Come back in here, Cassie.'

She crossed the corridor and knocked on the door.

'Come in, Cassie. Sit down,' he said.

She sat down in the chair opposite, her eyes bright and her notebook and pen at the ready.

Angel said, 'The murderer is using a lipstick colour called "Passion Pink" made by a manufacturer whose brand name is Honeymoon. I need to know how well represented that brand is in Bromersley, and in particular how easy it is to buy that specific colour. So I want you to do a quick survey of beauty shops, cosmetic shops, chemists, department stores . . . any place that sells cosmetics, and find out if they stock that particular brand, also if they have a lipstick of that specific colour for sale. All right?'

'Right, sir,' she said. Her bright eyes shone brighter. She was delighted to be sent on another inquiry.

'And it would be a good idea to buy one so that we can see what it looks like,' he added.

'Right, sir. I'll do that, if I can,' she said.

She rushed eagerly out of the office and closed the door.

Angel looked at his watch. It was only two o'clock.

He put on his hat and coat and went out of his office, up the corridor past the cells and out of the rear door to the car park.

Fountain Street was off Sheffield Road and had two large blocks of flats on it. One of them was called Montpelier House. He parked the BMW in front of the building and took the lift to the first floor. He soon found Flat 14 and he rang the bell.

A young woman opened the door.

Angel smiled at her and said, 'Can I see Mr Marx, please.'

'Oooh,' she said. 'Philip Marx hasn't lived here for ages.'

Angel heard the voice of a man somewhere behind the young woman say, 'Who is it, lass?'

She turned back to him. 'It's another one of them asking for Philip, Dad.'

The voice said, 'Tell him we don't know where he is and that we cannot be held responsible for his debts.'

Angel whipped out his ID. 'I'm not a debt collector, Miss. I'm a police inspector from the Bromersley force,' he said. 'I'm trying to get in touch with Mr Marx.'

A man appeared at the door wearing a shirt and trousers held up with red braces. He brushed the young woman to one side. 'So are twenty-five other folks, mate. He owes money all over the place.'

The young woman glared at him. 'You shouldn't *say* that, Dad. Just 'cos a few debt collectors have called looking for him . . .'

The man's eyebrows shot up. 'A *few*!' he said.

Angel said, 'Could I have your name, sir?'

'Yes. Dean Potts. We moved in here on 1 March, that's two weeks, nearly three weeks ago, and during that time I reckon there's been five men who have been at this door looking for him.'

'No. That's not right,' the daughter said. 'It's been *three* at the most.'

Potts turned to Angel and said, 'Take no notice of her. This is my daughter, Marcia. She's at that age when she gets the hots for anything in trousers under thirty. I can't understand it. And this chap . . . this Philip Marx, he had a face that looked as if he'd been hit by a flat iron.'

'He couldn't help his looks, Dad. He'd been assaulted by a gang of thugs. He was very nice.'

'Huh. That's what he *told* you,' her father said.

Angel turned to the man and said, 'Well, when was the last time you spoke to him, Mr Potts?'

'That would be the day we moved in, 1 March.'

'Did he leave a forwarding address or a phone number for his mail or whatever?'

'No. He said he'd call in, pick it up and see if we'd settled down all right.'

'And has there been any?'

'No,' Potts said.

'And has he called in,' Angel said.

'Not yet,' Potts said with a sniff.

'But he will,' Marcia Potts said firmly then glared at her father.

Angel licked his bottom lip then said, 'I see. You wouldn't have a photo of him Miss, would you?'

Potts said, 'She'd better not have.'

She glared at her father, then turned to Angel and said, 'No, Inspector I haven't.'

Angel said, 'Well, if he *does* call in to see you, be sure to let me know straightaway. It's very important.'

He reached into his pocket for a business card and put it into Potts' outstretched hand.

'Why?' Potts said. 'What's he done?'

'He is wanted for questioning,' Angel said, metaphorically crossing his fingers. He didn't think it prudent to be more explicit.

Angel thanked Mr Potts and his daughter, took his leave and arrived at the station at a few minutes to five.

He headed for his office to find in the middle of his desk under a stapling machine, a piece of paper with handwriting on it. It read: *To Inspector Angel. Please phone SOCO as soon as possible. Cassie Jagger (Cadet).*

He blinked. It must be important. He picked up the phone and tapped in a number.

'SOCO. DS Taylor. Can I help you?' a voice said.

'I have a message to phone you, Don,' Angel said.

'Ah, yes, sir. Got an email from the lab. It said that the DNA samples of the skin and hair of the assailant discovered on the bodies of the five victims are a perfect match.'

Angel's eyebrows went up. His face brightened. 'That confirms what we already thought. It means that the five murders were committed by the same person.'

'Yes, sir,' Taylor said. 'There's more. But it isn't helpful. The DNA doesn't identify anybody in the rogues gallery on the PNC.'

Angel looked down and rubbed his forehead with his fingertips. 'Another dead end,' he said.

He thanked Taylor and returned the phone to its cradle.

He looked at his watch. It said five o'clock. He'd had enough of that week. He was headed home.

* * *

Angel drove the BMW straight into the garage, pulled down the up and over door and went down the path to the back of the house and let himself in.

As soon as he opened the door, he could smell cooking. It was Friday. His nose told him it was to be salmon poached in butter, which was good news.

Mary walked in from the hall. She blinked and smiled. 'Oh it's you. I heard the door. You didn't call out.'

'Yes, it's me,' he said. 'Who were you expecting, Benedict Cumberbatch?'

She smiled.

He went up to her, took off his hat and gave her a peck on the cheek. Then went into the hall to hang up his hat and coat in the cubby hole space under the stairs.

'You're early,' she said.

'No, I'm not early, sweetheart. It's just that I am *not* late.'

She shrugged. 'Whatever. It's a change anyway. Tea will be about twenty-five minutes.'

'Great stuff,' he said. 'Any post,' he added, taking a can of beer out of the fridge.

Mary's face took on a pained look. 'You always ask me that. It's in the usual place.'

Angel frowned. 'Which is that? Sometimes it's on the mantel piece, sometimes on the sideboard, sometimes in your library book, sometimes in your handbag . . .'

'*All right! All right!* You know full well it's on the sideboard. And there's only one.'

Angel went into the sitting room. Sure enough on the sideboard was an envelope. He snatched it up. From all the advertising bumf printed on the outside it was obviously from the gas company. He ambled back to the kitchen as he tore open the envelope. He sniffed as he took out the content and opened it up. It was a bill. He glared at the bottom figure. His lips tightened back against his teeth.

Mary was grilling the sausages as he ambled back into the kitchen. 'Will you set the table, Michael?' she said.

'It's the gas bill,' he said.

She glanced up at the ceiling momentarily. 'I know!'

He saw her. He knew she had no patience with him anymore when it came to the gas company. He angrily stuffed the bill in to his shirt pocket and yanked open the cutlery drawer, quickly selected some cutlery. He slammed it shut. He banged each piece in position on the table. He reached into the cupboard for two tea plates and the salt and pepper pots. Then he went to a drawer in the cabinet and took out four table mats: two large and two small. He threw them at the table like he was dealing cards. They landed pretty well in position. He looked across the table to see if he had forgotten anything. Satisfied he hadn't, he darted into the hall, took off his coat, put it on a coat hanger in the cupboard under the stairs, banged the door shut, returned to the kitchen and made his way to the sink, just as Mary moved sideways from the oven to pour the leeks into a colander.

'What do you want?' Mary said.

'Wash my hands.'

'That's what the bathroom's for.'

'The bathroom's for having a bath.'

'And the kitchen's for cooking.'

'When you're upstairs you can wash your hands upstairs. When you're downstairs you can wash your hands in the kitchen.'

'*Not* when the meal is ready and the cook is serving up.'

'Well how long is the obstreperous, bad tempered, stunningly gorgeous cook going to be monopolising the sink?'

Angel noticed that she struggled not to smile.

'Just as long as it takes,' she said. 'Sit down. I'm almost ready to serve up.'

'No,' he said. 'I'm not going to eat my tea with unwashed hands.' He turned and made for the sitting room. 'I'll go and watch the telly. Let me know when I can get to the sink, will you?'

'Come back, you great fool,' she said, lifting the plates off the work top with an oven cloth. 'It's on the table. You can have the sink to yourself now, but your meal is going cold.'

Angel turned and came back. He washed his hands quickly and sat down to the meal.

They ate in silence which was unusual.

Angel enjoyed the salmon, had cleared his plate and when he had neatly put his knife and fork together he looked at his wife and said, 'Mary, I know you don't want to talk about it, but if we did, it would be better because it would clear the air.'

Mary swallowed the last piece of salmon then she reached over for Angel's plate which she put on top of hers and put them on the draining board. She picked up the prepared sweets and came back to the table with them.

'The trouble is Michael,' she said. 'I know *exactly* what you are going to say. You are going to say that the bill is too much. And I keep saying the same thing, that there's nothing we can do about it. If we want to cook our meals and keep warm in a modern, civilised way, we have to have gas. And we have to pay for it. There is no alternative.'

He shook his head. 'Mary, I was going to say that last year we shelled out four thousand pounds that we didn't have and had to borrow from our building society by sticking that amount back onto our mortgage, to buy a new boiler that was supposed to have saved us a minimum of thirty per cent on our bill. But our bills are *higher*. They aren't even the same. They are *much higher*!'

'But Michael, we had no choice. We had to have the new boiler because the other one packed up on us, didn't it? We didn't borrow the money to . . . er to spend on a cruise or anything like that. It was an urgent necessity.'

'That doesn't change the fact that they said that a modern boiler would *save* us about thirty percent. Instead the bills are about twenty-five percent higher.'

'Isn't that because we are using more?'

Angel put up a hand and rubbed his forehead with the tips of his fingers. She was wearing him down. His patience was exhausted. Resignedly he said, 'I haven't checked to see if we are using more.'

'I think it's a been a lot colder for a lot longer this winter than last, so we *would* have to pay more, wouldn't we?'

Angel rubbed his face hard with both his hands for a few seconds before he managed to say, 'Have you got a job with the gas people that you haven't yet told me about?'

For a moment, her mouth dropped open. She looked at his very serious face and then burst out laughing. 'Of course not,' she said intermingled with the laughter.

Angel seeing his wife's reaction, thought about what he had said, and broke out into a smile and then a chuckle. Their heads came together and then midst the hilarity they kissed on the lips.

Angel went into the sitting room, picked up the *Radio Times*, sat down in his usual easy chair and began to turn the page to the evenings programmes.

Mary followed with the coffees.

When they were both settled, he said, 'Had a good day?'

'Boring, boring, boring,' she said. 'You?'

'Put a bit more flesh on the bones of the murderer. He carries a lipstick, probably in his pocket, and has not been in trouble with the police recently.'

She blinked. 'What's this about a lipstick?'

He told her what Mac had discovered and reported to him earlier that day.

'I've never heard of Honeymoon cosmetics,' she said.

'Well, it'll be a small firm, I expect. What about the colour, "Passion Pink"? Have you heard of that?'

'It doesn't sound a modern, sophisticated name for a colour. They are simply making use of obvious, unimaginative alliteration.'

Angel's mouth dropped open. He was surprised. He wasn't used to Mary criticising *other* people. She usually saved it all for him.

‘Anyway,’ she continued, ‘what makes you say that the murderer will have the lipstick in his pocket?’

‘Well it may not be in his pocket, but it will be on his person somewhere. I say *that* because I think his murders are not always premeditated. He’s clearly well organised even if he is a psycho. And he’s boastful. He wants to claim credit for his crimes. And if he came across anybody who recognized him from the time before the operation on his face, he might very well decide to murder them before they could tell, and he’d want to have the lipstick handy.’

Mary shuddered. ‘Don’t talk like that, Michael. It’s so . . . erm, so cold blooded.’

‘Sorry, sweetheart. But this man *is* cold blooded.’

EIGHT

It was eight o'clock on Sunday evening, 20 March. It had been a pleasant Spring day but it was now dark and cold.

Mrs Buller-Price had had a most enjoyable day at her new home, the Monks' Retreat. She had been to church that morning, enjoyed a leisurely walk with the dogs round the lake, had a light lunch, and spent the rest of the day baking and cooking.

The dogs had also had a delightful day. They had enjoyed being outside most of the daylight hours, and since had enjoyed a hearty supper and were now in the sitting room, snoozing on the settee or on the Axminster, while Tulip, the cat, had found herself a spot she liked on the delft rack.

Mrs Buller-Price had finished her supper and was treating herself to a glass of Campions Ginger Wine. After a while, she cleared the table and carried the dirty dishes on a tray through to the kitchen. She put the tray down on the draining board of the sink intending to put the used pots and cutlery into soak, when the room light in the centre of the ceiling went out leaving the kitchen in complete darkness.

'Oh,' she said. 'Whatever's happened?'

There was a small amount of moonlight coming through the window, but her eyes were not yet accustomed to the darkened room. She carefully manoeuvred her way to the kitchen door that lead into the hall. She noted that the hall and the sitting room were also in total darkness. She tracked down the door jamb and found the light switch. She flicked it up and down a couple of times. Nothing happened.

'Must be a mains fuse or a power cut,' she said to herself, while standing there in the dark.

She looked at the watch on her wrist. She could see the luminous fingers and numbers on the dial. It said ten minutes past eight. She knew that it would be useless trying to get an electrician out at that time on a Sunday evening. She reconciled herself to dealing with the problem in daylight the following morning.

She fumbled her way round the downstairs rooms setting the light switches to the off position. She told the dogs to settle down for the night, put down a dish of water for them in the sitting room and closed the door.

She then made her way up the stairs, undressed in the dark and got into bed. She said her prayers silently from memory and added a request that that she might be assisted to repair the darkness in the house easily and inexpensively in the morning. Then she fell asleep.

She was enjoying a dream about touring the highlands of Scotland in an open top car with her dear husband and with two spaniels in the back, when one of the dogs began barking and wouldn't stop. She was worried that there was something wrong. She had repeatedly commanded the dog to be quiet but he would not. Her husband was beginning to be slightly put out by the persistent racket and walkers carrying backpacks that they passed were giving them strange looks. She turned round in her seat to investigate further and found that she was sitting up in bed in the dark at the Monks' Retreat and the dog causing the uproar was Schwarzenegger, her Great Dane, accompanied by Zsa Zsa, the Labrador and Bogart, the Heinz 57, who were downstairs in the sitting room.

The barking was repeated, louder and in bursts. It couldn't have come on a more unwelcome night, when the electricity had chosen to die on her. Schwarzenegger perhaps needed to 'spend a penny' or something else had disturbed him. He was usually a most quiet dog. Zsa Zsa, she was sure, was simply enjoying exercising her vocal chords, contributing lower notes to the chorus, and Bogart merely joining in with a higher yap.

Mrs Buller-Price fumbled around in the drawer in the bedside cabinet and found a small flashlight, placed there deliberately for such contingencies. She switched it on. It didn't put out much light. It really needed new batteries. She shook it to see if she could get a stronger light, but it was not to be. She pointed it at the clock and it said 2 a.m. She switched the flashlight off to save the battery. She whisked back the bedclothes, found her slippers and dressing-gown, put them on and made her way in darkness to the door, along the landing to the big staircase. The dogs must have heard her because the barking became louder with increased enthusiasm as she progressed along the hall to the sitting room. She was pleased that she didn't have any neighbours because the racket the dogs were making at that time of the night would certainly have been grounds for complaint.

She reached the door, switched on the flashlight, turned the knob and pushed open the door. All three dogs rushed up to greet her, panting and wagging their tails. The two biggest dogs stopped barking. They sniffed around searching for her hands so that they could lick them. She pointed the flashlight round the room.

'What's all this noise about? You should be asleep, not making all this racket. Do you need to go out?'

There were muted but enthusiastic small barks from the two big dogs that indicated that they did. Bogart yapped at her ankles which indicated that he did also.

She suddenly noticed the little red standby light on the television. She stared at it and frowned. 'That wouldn't be lit if the power was cut off,' she muttered.

She reached out to the wall, found the light switch, and suddenly there was light. She smiled and went out into the hall accompanied by the dogs, and tried the other switches. The lights came on. Everything seemed to be in order. She sighed with relief.

Then Schwarzenegger's ears pricked up. He growled then barked and continued barking, accompanied by Zsa Zsa and Bogart. After a while, they stopped barking, and Schwarzenegger stood stock still and inclined his head to one side for a few seconds seemingly to listen.

Watching these antics, Mrs Buller-Price deduced that Schwarzenegger could hear someone or something unfamiliar to him, and therefore probably unknown to her, and certainly not welcome there at this time of night.

The Great Dane pushed past her. He urgently wanted to get out of the sitting room. He stopped, came back, looked back at her then trotted out through the front hall, with Zsa Zsa and Bogart following, right up to the front door.

Mrs Buller-Price was compelled to join the procession.

When they all arrived, the three dogs looked up at her. Schwarzenegger pawed the door.

The old lady had to consider what to do.

The dogs began barking again. The row was deafening. Clearly Schwarzenegger could hear some activity of some sort. At that time in the early morning, under a pitch black sky, it must be something nefarious.

Now Mrs Buller-Price adored her dogs. She didn't want anything to happen to them, but something should be done. She didn't feel brave enough to deal with it herself. She could ring the police but it might take 30 minutes for them to arrive even if they were in a position to answer the call promptly.

'No gang. You can't go out. No,' she said.

They glanced at her and began dancing round the door. She put her hand on the door lock. The barking and dancing increased.

'I don't want you being hurt, you know. I'm going to open the door to see what's happening. You stay where you are, do you hear? All three of you. Stay. *Stay.*'

She reached up to the wall and switched on the outside lights. She opened the door slightly and peered cautiously out into the night.

She had switched on two floodlights that illuminated the entire frontage of the house up to the edge of the lake, including the tiny boathouse, but there was no sign of life.

Schwarzenegger looked at Zsa Zsa and the pair of them pushed round Mrs Buller-Price's legs almost knocking her down. Then they squeezed their way through the partly opened door, forcing it open wider, and before she realised what was happening, they were through it and had disappeared into darkness.

The heavy brick she suddenly felt in her chest banged rapidly like a drum.

'Bad dogs! Bad dogs! Come back! Come back!' she called. 'Schwarzenegger! Zsa Zsa! Come back!'

But they were gone. She looked round for Bogart. He was at her feet, dancing around. He was looking for a way out. As she bent down to pick him up, he pushed his way between her legs so that he was suddenly behind her. She quickly turned round. But he had disappeared though the open door and was gone.

Her eyes flashed. 'Bogart, come back here this instant!' she called, but it was too late. He was out of sight.

She gritted her teeth and shook her head. All her chins wobbled.

She stepped outside several metres and looked in the direction the dogs had taken. 'You bad dogs. All three of you! Disgraceful!' Then in a softer voice she said, 'You must be very careful, and look after each other.'

The barking continued in the distance.

The three dogs, led by Schwarzenegger knew exactly where they were going. They raced to the right, behind a privet fence, past the garages to the main entrance in the stone wall around the big house. It consisted of two big, high wooden doors that had a door for pedestrians in one of them.

Mrs Buller-Price returned to the front door and was holding her dressing-gown across her chest. She wished she could know what was happening. She could see nothing, but could hear plenty. The dogs were on target within seconds. A right old skirmish began with human male voices expressing their alarm with a series of 'Ohs', 'hooos', 'ahhhhs' and 'get off me.'

Then she heard both the gnashing of Schwarzenegger's and Zsa Zsa's teeth combined with their angry growling, while little Bogart maintained a continual high pitched yapping.

Suddenly there was a scream from a man followed by a tirade of expletives. Then the sound of a car door being slammed. Then another barrage of barking from all three dogs. A moment later, she heard the sound of a motor vehicle starting up and pulling away quickly. The sound of it soon faded into the darkness of the night. After a few moments, the barking ceased.

Mrs Buller-Price thought that that sounded as if the intruders had gone. She hoped her dogs were unhurt in the fracas.

Moments later, the dogs came trotting back to Mrs Buller-Price standing in the doorway. She looked down at them eagerly. All three had their heads up and tails wagging, which was a good sign.

She leaned forward to examine each of the dogs to see if they had been injured in any way.

It was pointless chastising them at that point. She knew that if she did, it would have seemed to them that she was not pleased to see them return.

Schwarzenegger seemed to be in fine fettle.

Zsa Zsa pushed in for some attention. Mrs Buller-Price patted her on her head and down her back. As she tried to feel down each of her legs, Zsa Zsa kept pushing her mouth towards her hand. Eventually, she dropped a small squishy piece of dark blue fabric into it. It must be something she had come across during the skirmish at the main gate. She wagged her tail and gave a small bark.

The old lady frowned and pursed her lips as she stretched out the trophy. It was about two centimetres by eight, frayed around all the edges as if it had been torn from a man's suit, probably the trousers.

* * *

The following morning at 8.45 a.m., the office phone rang out.

He reached out for it. 'DI Angel,' he said.

'Sergeant Clifton, sir. Control Room. Just had a triple nine, and the super is away in London.'

'Yes. Yes,' Angel said quickly. 'All right, Bernie. What is it?'

'It's from a Mr Alexander Moore of an advertising agency in Inkerman Street in Old Town.'

Angel blinked. His mouth dropped open. He wondered what could possibly be wrong there. 'Yes, Bernie, what's up?'

'He's just reported an unexplained death. He actually used the word murder, sir. He said that a member of his staff has been found dead in the company car park. I've sent a patrol car to assist.'

Angel felt his pulse beat faster. His chest tightened. He closed his eyes briefly. He didn't want to believe that yet another person had been murdered. He had never known such a prolific waste of human life in the town. He ran a hand through his hair.

He rang off then quickly alerted SOCO, Dr Mac, DS Flora Carter and Inspector Asquith.

Then he rang DS Clifton in the Control Room back. 'What's the super doing in London, Bernie?'

'He's gone to the Gift Fair, sir. I understand that he's looking for prizes for the darts competition.'

Angel's eyes rolled up to the ceiling. 'Right, Bernie,' he said and he replaced the receiver.

A few moments later, Flora Carter came in. 'Is it another one of the lipstick murders, sir?'

'I don't know, Flora. But I wouldn't be a bit surprised.'

'What do you want me to do, sir?'

Angel rubbed his chin.

There was a knock at the door.

Angel called, 'Come in.'

It was Cadet Jagger. She was holding out her notebook. 'Am I interrupting, sir?'

'No,' Angel said. 'No. Come in.'

Flora looked at the girl and nodded.

She acknowledged the nod and said, 'Sergeant.'

'Sit down, Cassie,' Angel said then he looked back at Flora. 'I'll be going out there shortly. I want you to come with me. Don't go far. I'll give you a ring.'

'Right, sir,' Flora said and she went out.

When the door closed, Angel turned to the cadet and said, 'Have you completed that inquiry about lipstick stockists?'

'Yes, sir,' she said consulting her notebook. 'There were thirteen outlets that stocked cosmetics in and around Bromersley. I called on each one and only two stocked the Honeymoon brand. One was a little shop, Baileys, in the inside market and the other was Cheapo's, the supermarket. Both retailers had stocks of Honeymoon's "Passion Pink" lipstick. I bought one from the little shop run by a Mrs Bailey for £3.75. The price at Cheapo's was £4. 39.'

Angel held out his hand.

She passed the lipstick over to him. It was in a gold coloured case with a black base. Angel looked under the base and saw the words *Passion Pink* printed in black on a gilt coloured sticker. He slid it out of its case to reveal a black plastic holder. He pushed the button at the side to expose the vivid red stick. He looked at it, frowned and said, 'And women pay £3.75 for *that*?'

Cassie said, 'Oh yes, sir. You can pay up to £40 or more for some brands.'

His eyebrows shot up. He was thinking. He leaned back in the chair and rubbed his chin. He hoped that Mary wasn't shelling out that sort of money simply to colour her lips.

* * *

An hour passed and Angel couldn't wait any longer. He reached for the phone and told Flora Carter to meet him outside at his car straightaway.

She jumped in the BMW quickly and he drove to the Old Town district of Bromersley. When they arrived at Inkerman Street, there were cars parked on both sides of the road. Up the short drive to the Moore and Moore building were four police vehicles parked together. There was just enough room for another car in the drive so he parked behind them. They all had blue lights flashing on their roofs. Although he had seen the insistent blue lights flickering hundreds of times they always unnerved him. As they got out of the car, he turned to the sergeant and said, 'Flora, after we've seen Don Taylor, make a note of all those car numbers in the street and find out the owners. Can't imagine where they've all come from.'

'Right, sir.'

As they walked towards the crime scene, they saw that a small part of the otherwise empty car park for Moore & Moore staff and visitors, which was at the side of the building, was partly covered by a small white tent or canopy. It was marked off with POLICE — DO NOT ENTER tape around it.

That probably explained why Inkerman Street was jam-packed with cars.

Angel wrinkled his nose. He was to have to look at another dead body. There were occasions when he wondered why he was a policeman, and this was one of them.

'Come on then, Flora,' he said. 'Let's get this over with.'

They crossed the road and went up to the tape. A uniformed constable saluted him. Angel reciprocated.

At that moment, a SOC's man in a white suit, boots, hat and mask came out of the tent carrying a white bag. He was headed to the SOC van which was among the police vehicles parked up the drive.

'Is DS Taylor there, lad?' Angel said.

'He's in the tent, sir. I'll get him for you?' He turned back and went into the tent. He could hear several exchanges between him and Taylor. The man returned carrying two slim white packets.

'He's sent these gloves, sir,' the man said, 'and he says he'll be out directly.'

'Right. Thank you,' Angel said.

Angel and Flora tore open the packets and put on the rubber gloves.

Taylor whipped back a flap in the tent, looked round, saw Angel and Carter standing by the tape and came up to them.

'Couldn't wait any longer, Don?' Angel said.

Taylor knew his boss too well. He nodded and lifted the tape. 'We're not *quite* finished, sir.'

Angel nodded and said, 'Let's be having a look. See what's happened.'

They followed Taylor into the small tent.

The scene was brightly illuminated by two spotlights.

Angel saw that there were three other forensic men and women in their disposable sterile whites. There were working shoulder to shoulder around a car in unusually cramped conditions.

Angel's eyes zoomed to the centre of their attention. It was the body of a man on his back laid across the bonnet of a car. His face was drained of blood. He had the word JUDAS daubed in red on his forehead. He was about 30, had long hair and an earring in his left ear. His mouth slightly open and his eyes closed. He was wearing jeans and a red jersey under a duffle coat partly buttoned up.

Angel immediately recognized the dead man. A sudden coldness hit him in the stomach. He squeezed his eyes shut.

'It's Nigel Hobbs,' he said.

Taylor blinked. 'Yes, sir,' he said.

'He was a copywriter here at Moore's,' Angel said.

Flora stared at him. 'You *knew* him, sir?'

Angel sighed. 'Interviewed him on Friday,' he said. 'He was a bit odd then.' He recalled that Hobbs was still upset because he thought he should have visited Phil Marx, or Arrowsmith his alias, in the hospital more often.

Flora's eyes narrowed. She was puzzled.

Angel looked at Taylor. 'Who found him, Don?'

'Two other members of staff, sir. They're in the offices waiting for you.'

He nodded. 'Hasn't Doctor Mac arrived?'

Mac was at the other side of the car. He looked across the body. 'I'm here, Michael,' he said, looking up. 'I've done everything I need to do here.'

He had been bending down packing up his bag.

'Oh?' Angel said. 'What have you got, Mac?'

'Not much,' he said. 'You'll have seen his forehead? I'll check that that lipstick is the same as the others. The victim has a large contusion on the back of the head, so I suggest — nothing more, Michael, than I *suggest* — that he must have received a severe blow from the proverbial blunt instrument which had caused him to lose consciousness, then he was physically asphyxiated. You can actually see ecchymoses on the throat—'

Angel frowned. 'Ecchymoses? What's that? Come off it, Mac.'

Mac's jaw muscles tightened. 'All right,' he said. 'You can actually see the contusions . . . the *bruising* on his throat caused by the fingers and thumbs being applied excessively. It is simply known in the trade as ecchymoses.'

Angel looked more closely at the throat of the dead man. He nodded. Then he rubbed his chin and said, 'Ecchymoses? You've made it up, Mac.'

'I have nae.'

Angel said, 'Same method used on the four women?'

'Aye. Exactly.'

'Have you the time of death?'

'Och, between two hours and three hours ago.'

'That's between 7.30 and 8.30.' Angel looked at the sergeant. 'Did you get that, Flora?'

Mac said, 'I can't tell you anything else until I have him on the table.'

Angel said, 'Thanks, Mac.'

Then Angel turned to Flora and said, 'Off you go. See if anybody saw anything around that time. All the houses that have an unrestricted view of the scene. It could be vital. And get the car registration numbers afterwards.'

She knew the importance of the mission. She nodded and dashed off.

Angel came out of the tent shortly afterwards on to the car park. He walked across to the front door of Moore & Moore's. He asked the receptionist to see whoever had found the dead man. She showed him into an interview room near the reception. It was small with only three chairs and a table.

Angel pulled out a chair and sat down ready for action.

Moments later, Moore looked through the open door and came in. His face was drawn and he had grey patches under his eyes.

'I saw you arrive, Inspector,' Moore said. 'Oh dear. Oh dear, Inspector. Whatever next?'

Angel shrugged. He thought the same. He didn't have an answer for him.

Moore said, 'Is this room satisfactory for you, Inspector? If there's anything you want, please say.'

'It's fine, Mr Moore. It's fine, thank you.'

'I'll leave you to it, then,' he said.

Moore went out and then came back. 'Would you like a some tea or coffee?'

'No thank you.'

Eventually Moore left Angel with his thoughts and shortly afterwards, a man about 30, tapped on the open door.

'Inspector Angel? I'm Adam Quinn. I was the one who . . . found Nigel . . . Nigel Hobbs.'

Angel looked up. 'Oh yes. Come in, Mr Quinn. Sit down.'

Quinn closed the door and pulled up a chair.

'Please tell me what you saw.'

'It's simple enough, Inspector. We start work at half past eight. I suppose it was about eight twenty when I arrived. I saw that Nigel's car was already in the car park. His and Mr Moore's. I pulled my car up next to his and as I got out I noticed a figure of somebody on the bonnet. I rushed round and saw that it was Nigel. He looked ghastly. I saw the word *Judas* written on his forehead and realised that he must be another victim of the lipstick murderer I had read about. At that moment another car arrived. It was Teresa Scott. She saw me and . . . and we looked at Nigel . . . and I suppose we both took it for granted that he was dead. We went straight to Mr Moore, who phoned 999. That's about it.'

Angel nodded and said, 'Did you see anybody around the car park or on the street when you arrived?'

'No. There was nobody. It was pretty quiet. Usually is, on Inkerman Street at this time in the morning.'

Angel finished his questioning of Adam Quinn, then he saw Teresa Scott and she confirmed all that Quinn had said. He then interviewed Tom Skerritt, manager of the creative department of the agency.

'No, I don't know of any disputes in the creative department or in the company,' Skerritt said.

'Have you had any staff changes recently?'

'We're *always* having staff changes,' Skerritt said. 'They come and they go. We're always running on three legs. A clerk in the accounts office left at Christmas. We had our best accounts' executive leave a month ago. They've only just been replaced. In my department we had a copywriter leave us in January, and he was only replaced last week. That's the man you've just interviewed. All that time, we were managing with only one copywriter. I had to prepare the copy for some of the accounts, with the help of Mr Moore. Then we got Adam Quinn. He's all right but I have to show him the ropes. Now that Nigel Hobbs has gone means that I'm one copywriter down *again*.'

Angel rubbed his chin. His heart began to race. His eyes moved slowly from side to side as he considered the latest information. How clever it would be if the murderer, who he believed was Philip Marx or Frank Arrowsmith came back to Moore & Moore with a new face and got his job back as a copywriter under *another* assumed name.

'This man, Adam Quinn,' Angel said. 'What do you know about him?'

Skerritt said, 'He came highly recommended from an advertising agency in Lancashire somewhere, where he had worked as a copywriter for more than 10 years, I think they said. Mr Moore has his history.'

'Thank you, Mr Skerritt. You may have helped more than you know.'

Skerritt stood up and went out, and Angel promptly went to see Mr Moore in his office.

'Quinn seemed a good man to have on the team,' Moore said. 'He came from a big agency in Manchester, *Porter Publicity*. I have a letter of recommendation of him from them in his file.'

Moore found the letter and handed it to Angel. He read it. It spoke well of Quinn and it confirmed that he had been in their employ for 10 years.

Angel took a note of the phone number of Porter Publicity and the name of the writer, Gilbert Porter.

Then Angel suddenly said, 'Do you have Quinn's date of birth, Mr Moore?'

'Date of birth, Inspector?' Moore said with a frown. He reached down to a drawer and took out a ledger.

'It'll help with identification,' Angel said.

Moore was looking through his wages book. 'It's a question we always ask,' he said. 'I will have it somewhere . . . here it is: 6 December 1988.'

'Thank you,' Angel said. He made a note of it. He remembered. It was St Nicolas day.

He handed the letter back to Moore and said, 'Who are the other two employees who joined you in the past week or so?'

'There's Harry Simms, he looks to be a good man. He's to replace an accounts executive. He worked in sales. We couldn't find a man experienced in advertising so we will have to train him. And then there's Alan Stone. He's a sales support clerk.'

Angel carefully wrote down their names. He needed to see them both very soon. One of them could be Philip Marx, the murderer of Nigel Hobbs. If it could be shown that he murdered Hobbs, then he also murdered five other innocent people.

Angel's mobile phone rang. 'Excuse me, Mr Moore.'

Moore nodded and said, 'Go ahead, Inspector.'

He delved into his pocket and pulled out his mobile. It was Cassie Jagger.

'A lady rang, sir. Mrs Buller-Price. She sounded very upset. She said she had a problem and could she come and speak to you about it. I told her you were out but that you were expected back sometime soon. She said she would call in straightaway and hoped that it would be convenient. I didn't make any promises, sir. I hope that that is all right?'

'That's all right, Cassie. I'm about finished here anyway. I won't be long.'

He closed the phone, stood up, thanked Moore and said, 'Something urgent has cropped up. But I will be back as soon as I can.'

As he drove smartly towards the station, he wondered about dear Mrs Buller-Price. There was always something going wrong.

He pressed the car as legally fast as he could manage. As he changed up to top gear and turned onto the ring road, his mind turned to back to thinking about the murders. He couldn't understand why Arrowsmith or Marx (or whatever new alias he had lately assumed) had killed Nigel Hobbs.

The man had killed the doctor, the nurse and the tea girl to maintain his anonymity; the murder of his ex-girlfriend,

Sarah Steadman, seemed like revenge; and her mother, Cora possibly because she caught him in the act of murdering Sarah; but the killing of Nigel Hobbs didn't make sense. And the murderer hadn't even attempted to conceal the fact that he had committed the act. On the contrary, he had left his signature: the lipstick writing of *Judas* on the dead man's forehead.

NINE

Angel stood up as Cassie Jagger showed Mrs Buller-Price into his office.

'Come in, Mrs Buller-Price,' Angel said. 'How very nice to see you again. Please sit down.'

Mrs Buller-Price smiled and sat down on the chair facing him. She lowered her capacious bag to the floor and put the umbrella with the duck's head handle across her knees.

Cassie stood by the door and looked at Angel hoping to catch his eye. She did and with a hand gesture he indicated that she should stay and observe. She closed the door and made for the other chair next to the stationery cupboard.

Mrs Buller-Price then reached down to her very large bag and took out a silver foil dish wrapped over with transparent cling film and said, 'Last time I saw you, Inspector, I told you I would bring you a gooseberry fool. And here it is.'

She put it on the desk in front of him.

Angel beamed. He had tasted her cooking before. She could cook for England. 'That's extremely kind of you, Mrs Buller-Price. Thank you.'

She returned the beam, then reached back down to the bag and took out a white envelope which she held tightly between fingers and thumb.

'What else have you got?' Angel said.

She told him of her experiences in the early hours of that morning. Then she leaned forward, pushed the envelope across his desk and said, 'In there is a piece of cloth that my dog, Zsa Zsa, came back with. How can I be sure that she didn't bite one of them causing a flesh wound, and what would I do if the recipient of any such bite came looking to me for damages or worse, caught rabies?'

Angel smiled. 'My dear Mrs Buller-Price, as the person or persons were clearly trespassing on private property in the dead of night — although we have no idea what they were up to — it's hardly likely that they would come forward and reveal themselves to complain about been bitten by the householder's dog. They are far more likely to remember your dogs and not return to be assaulted by them a second time, aren't they?'

Mrs Buller-Price shook her head, sighed, then beamed. 'You know, Inspector, it is always a comfort to talk to you,' she said. 'You always simplify things and point out the logic of the situation in quick sticks. I have been chewing this round in my mind most of this morning thinking the very worst could happen, and in no time at all, you sort it out, simplify it and point out that there is nothing to worry about.'

As she was speaking, he had opened the envelope and peered at the piece of suiting.

'It certainly looks like it came from a man's suit,' he said as he rubbed his chin. 'That's the second time you've had strange happenings in your new home. Was there anything else you haven't mentioned?'

'Oh yes,' she said. 'At about eight o'clock in the evening, all the lights in the house went out. I thought it might be a fuse. Anyway later on they came in by themselves.'

'That *is* odd,' he said. 'Have you any ideas what the intruders wanted? You haven't anything valuable in the house, have you?'

She shook her chins. Then she said, 'I have my husband's golf clubs. They are worth a hundred or two, I suppose.'

'No. I mean more valuable than that.'

She pursed lips, pushed them forward, half closed her eyes and said, 'No, Inspector. And if you will excuse me, last night's episode was the *first*. I think that what happened *last* Monday night/Tuesday morning was all in my mind.'

'But there was that little plaque that one of your dogs found.'

'Yes, but it could have been there years.'

'Besides that, you saw two monks in that little rowing boat.'

'Ah,' she said. 'I now believe that that was a dream or a vision from the past.'

Angel shrugged. He put a hand up to his forehead and rubbed it with the tips of his fingers. He didn't think that it was as she had suggested.

Then he said, 'Mrs Buller-Price, please don't be offended by what I am going to ask you. A few people, from time to time, have told me things that . . . erm, shall we say . . . that were a bit fantastical. And they have sometimes been explained by side effects of a drug that they have been quite responsibly prescribed by their GP. Have you been taking any different pills since you moved house?'

Mrs Buller-Price blinked, then shook her chins and said, 'Indeed not, dear Inspector, I am pleased to say that I haven't had need to see my GP for almost a year now. I am as strong as a horse and twice as healthy.'

Angel smiled. 'I must say, you look it.' Then he went on to say, 'Anyway, to complete the story, when they stopped taking the drug, the dreams or visions passed.'

'Ah, no, not me,' she said. 'Not guilty.'

'I've also known it happen to those who have had too much to drink,' he said, 'but I have never seen *you* under the influence.'

That made her think. She didn't drink much at all. She didn't even drink every day. But occasionally she had imbibed a glass or two of Campions Ginger Wine. The bottle she found when she moved out of the farmhouse must have been at least twelve years old. She wondered if the ageing process had increased its potency and accentuated its effect on her. She made up her mind that the first thing she was going to do when she reached home, she was going to pour the rest of the bottle down the sink.

She smiled and said, 'Well, Inspector, thank you for listening to me.' She reached down for her bag on the floor and then stood up. 'I am very happy to leave the matter there.'

Angel stood up and said, 'Well, if you experience any further incident, please let me know, even if you think it might be a dream or a vision or whatever.'

'I certainly will, Inspector. I certainly will.'

As soon as Cassie and Mrs Buller-Price had left his office, Angel checked his notes, found the phone number of Porter Publicity in Manchester and tapped it into the phone. It was soon speaking to Gilbert Porter, creative director of the family business.

Angel explained who he was and why he was making inquiries about Adam Quinn, then he said, 'Was he working for you in December 2012?'

That was the Christmas Marx was assaulted in Bromersley and almost lost his life.

'He certainly was, Inspector,' Porter said. 'He was a very good copywriter. He worked here about ten years. We were sorry to lose him.'

Angel nodded. That put Quinn in the clear.

Angel said, 'Just one more question, Mr Porter. What is Adam Quinn's date of birth?'

Porter said, 'His date of birth? I don't have that at my fingertips. Hold on while I go through to another office.'

Angel remembered it. The year was 1988 and the month and day was St Nicolas day, 6 December, the day that some countries celebrate Christmas.

Porter was gone a minute or so then he came back. 'I've got it. Sorry about that. It is 6 December 1988.'

'Thank you, Mr Porter. Goodbye.'

Angel was pleased with the result of his questioning. It now meant that he had only two suspects.

When Cassie had carefully seen Mrs Buller-Price to her car she dashed back to Angel who was waiting in his overcoat and hat by his office door.

'Take that envelope with that piece of the intruder's trousers in it to Don Taylor, Cassie. Tell him what it is and how we came by it. Ask him if it is possible to get any forensic from it. I'm going back to Moore and Moore's.'

'Right, sir.'

* * *

The pretty young receptionist said, 'Mr Moore said you were coming, Inspector. He said you could use the interview room you had before, if you needed to.'

'Thank you,' Angel said. 'You have a recent member of your staff called Harry Simms. Would you be kind enough to ask him to join me?'

'Yes, of course.'

Angel went into the interview room next to Mr Moore's office and left the door open. He sat down at the small desk and waited. He pulled out the pocket recording machine, switched it on and put it on the desk in front on him. He rubbed his chin very slowly and hard, as he thought about the questions he was to put to Harry Simms.

After a moment or two, a man appeared at the door. He peered in. 'Inspector Angel?' he said.

Angel stood up. The man appeared to be in his thirties, in a smart dark suit, blue and white striped shirt and tie. 'Yes, Mr Harry Simms? Please come in.'

'No, sir,' the young man said. 'I'm the other newbie, Alan Stone. Mandy on reception said that Harry Simms isn't at his desk, so she thought she'd save you time. She knew you also wanted to see me. Is that all right?'

Angel frowned. He rubbed his chin again. It must be all round the building that he wanted to interview those particular two men this afternoon.

'Yes, of course,' he said. 'Come in. Please sit down.'

As Stone sat down, Angel noticed his hands on the chair arms. On the middle finger of his right hand was a red scar indicating a very recent injury. It was like a sudden jolt of electricity going through his body. He instantly recalled Sybil Roberts telling Cassie that her friend Tracey Thorne had told her that Arrowsmith had had a finger bandaged as well as his head.

Angel controlled his breathing. He was determined not to give anything away. He indicated the pocket recording machine. 'To save time, Mr Stone, I'm recording the interview. Can you tell me where you were this morning between seven thirty and eight thirty?'

'Yes, Inspector. That's easy,' Stone said. 'I got up about seven fifteen, I was in my flat getting washed, shaved, dressed and having my breakfast. At eight ten, I came out of the flat, got in my car and arrived here at around twenty or twenty-five past, to be at my desk by half past eight.'

'Can anybody vouch for that, or are you going to tell me you live on your own?'

Stone smiled. 'I am going to tell you I live on my own, Inspector.'

'That's *not* good news, Mr Stone,' Angel said. 'Where do you live?'

Stone frowned. 'Flat 11, Britannia House, Britannia Street, Bromersley,' he said. 'What do you want to know *that* for?'

'What do you think?' Angel said, fishing in his pocket for his mobile.

Stone smiled again. 'My first thought was that you are looking for a flatmate and wanted to share to save on the cost,' he said. 'You know, two can live as cheaply as one.'

Angel scrolled down his library of numbers, found SOCO's, and clicked on it.

As it rang out, he looked up at Stone he said, 'It's a very kind invitation but I have a house of my own and a wife to look after.'

Stone gave him a wry smile.

Into the phone he said, 'DS Taylor, please . . . ah, Don. Will you get a squad together to search the flat of Mr Alan Stone. The address is—'

Stone suddenly changed. His face was scarlet. '*You can't do that*,' he bawled. 'Why would you want to search where I live?'

The muscles on Angel's face tightened. Into the phone he said, 'Just a minute, Don.' He turned to Stone and said, 'I am looking into the murder of six innocent people. There are several reasons why you have become a suspect. A most important one is that you can't prove where you were at the time that Nigel Hobbs was murdered. Now you can allow us to search your flat unhindered or you can force us to obtain a warrant. Either way the end result will be the same. Also I will require you to come down to the station with me now.'

'What for? I've done nothing.'

'Maybe not, Mr Stone. But these matters are not very irksome for an innocent man. Now what do you want to do? Do you want to cooperate?'

'I suppose so,' he said. 'But I want to see my brief as soon as possible.'

A bell immediately rang in Angel's head.

The use of that word 'brief' immediately told Angel that he was talking to an ex jailbird. 'Brief' was the generic word used by villains who had been in trouble with the law, been through the courts and served time. An innocent member of the public caught up accidentally in some villainy of this sort would have been more likely to have said 'solicitor'. Angel thought that at last he was making progress.

'I will organise that as soon as we get to the station,' he said.

* * *

Angel was back in his office at the station. It was ten minutes past four. He was sat at his computer. He tapped in the password to the PNC followed by the name of Alan Stone and up came a picture of the man.

'Ah,' Angel said, 'an old customer of ours.' He scrolled downward and discovered that Stone was unmarried, in the RAF, that he was stationed at RAF Shawbury in Shropshire, for some time and later at Yeovilton in Somerset. Towards the end of his service in Yeovilton, he was found guilty of stealing a car and in possession of pair of stolen Georgian silver candlesticks and was given three years in prison at Taunton Crown Court in 2005, nothing known since.

Angel reckoned that he could very well be the man he was looking for. He must organise the cross examination of him.

He reached out for the phone and tapped in a number. 'Mr Bloomfield? I have a gentleman here. Name of Alan Stone. He urgently needs your representation. He asked for you by name.'

Bloomfield hesitated. 'Erm . . . what have you charged him with, Inspector?'

'Nothing yet. He is . . . assisting us with our inquiries.'

'Well, what are you *expecting* to charge him with?'

'There is a serious likelihood that we will charge him with murder.'

'Oh, I see,' Bloomfield said. 'I will come at once, Inspector.'

Angel replaced the phone. He went into the charge room where a PC had just finished taking Stone's fingerprints and was packing up the ink block and the cards.

'See that copies of those are given to DS Taylor in the SOC office, Constable. They need checking with those on the PNC,' Angel said.

'Right, sir,' he said as he went out.

Angel looked at Stone who was now dressed in blue denims and a blue shirt. His own clothes had been bagged up and labelled for examination by SOCO.

Stone turned and looked away.

Angel said, 'Mr Bloomfield is on his way here now. He seems to have heard of you.'

Stone didn't turn round. He didn't reply.

A man in a white coat came in carrying a small tray. On the tray was a small stainless bowl and a pair of rubber gloves. He looked across at Angel and hesitated.

Angel said, 'That's all right, lad. Carry on. Don't mind me.'

Stone turned, curious to know who had come in. He saw the man with the tray and said, 'What's all this?'

The man took the lid off the bowl and took out a glass bottle with a piece of cotton wool secured to a glass rod which was fastened to the inside of the stopper. He loosened the stopper and approached the prisoner. 'I have to take a buccal swab from you, that's all.'

Stone's eyes flashed. 'You're not doing that to me,' he said.

Angel said, 'Look Mr Stone, I know this is new to you, but it's nothing at all. He merely wants to wipe a piece of cotton wool across the inside of your mouth. It only takes a second or two and it doesn't hurt a bit.'

'What's it for?'

'It'll be sent to the lab to establish your DNA, that's all,' Angel said.

'Open your mouth,' the PC in the white coat said.

Stone looked at the PC and the cotton wool on the end of the glass rod and grudgingly opened his mouth.

The procedure was over in several seconds. The PC put the swab in the bottle and deftly secured the stopper in the glass tube with sticky tape. He asked Stone how he spelled his name, labelled the bottle, added the date and time, picked up the tray and went out.

Angel smiled. The result of that swab will tell him unequivocally whether Stone is the murderer or not, but it will take a month or longer.

The detective gave a big, involuntary sigh of satisfaction and went out of the charge room down the corridor to his office.

* * *

Ten minutes later Angel was in the A and E department of the hospital. It was a hive of activity. Doctors, nurses and ambulance staff dashing hither and thither.

He eventually managed to see Dr Armstrong who was the senior duty doctor.

Angel introduced himself, showed the doctor his ID then said, 'It may sound an unusual request, doctor, but have you had a man come in during the past 15 hours or so with an injury that might be described as a dog bite, who may have asked for an anti-tetanus jab?'

Doctor Armstrong frowned.

Angel continued, 'He may not have declared that the injury was caused by an animal. You see the man was one of several that I am looking for who was on private premises, in the middle of the night, alarming an elderly woman who lives on her own in a house in an isolated location. Her pet dogs were trying to protect her and it *is* possible that one or more of the intruders may have been bitten by one of them.'

The doctor's eyebrows went up. 'Ah yes,' he said. 'There was a man. Just a minute, I'll find the nurse who attended to him. You'll not keep her long, will you? We are very busy. Stay here. I'll send her to you as soon as she's free. I'll have to get back. Excuse me.'

Dr Armstrong rushed away.

A few minutes later a pretty young nurse came up to him. An ID badge on her uniform read *Nurse Naomi Jacobs*. She smiled and looked at the sheet of paper she was holding. 'Dr Armstrong said that you wanted to speak to me about a patient who needed an anti-tetanus jab earlier today,' she said.

Angel nodded. 'Yes. That's right, nurse. What can you tell me?'

She looked at the treatment sheet she was holding.

'Well, Triage passed him to me at 9.15 this morning,' she said. 'The patient said that he was bending down fixing an old, rusty gate, the wind blew it shut while he was in the way. I didn't believe him because I could see a set of teeth marks, about seven, both upper and lower, on the fleshy part of the top of his leg. I bathed the wounds with saline, then I gave him a muscular injection of tetanus immunoglobulin, to be on the safe side.'

'Have you his name and address?'

She referred to the paper again. 'Yes. Jameson, J., 111 Brook Street, Bromersley S78 1QY,' she said.

Angel beamed. 'Thank you very much indeed,' he said and quickly scribbled it down in his notebook. 'And what did he look like?'

'He was a big man. He gave his age as 53 years. Didn't say much.'

'Did he have any distinguishing features?'

She frowned and said, 'No. I don't think so.'

'Would you recognize him if you saw a photograph of him?'

She wrinkled her nose and turned down the corners of her mouth. Angel thought that she didn't like thinking about him.

'Oh yes,' she said confidently. 'Definitely.'

Angel's eyes glowed. He could have kissed her. She was pretty enough. But he didn't. 'Thank you *very much*,' he said.

* * *

Angel drove the BMW out of the hospital car park towards Park Road. He knew that Brook Street was off Park Road somewhere on the right. He eventually saw the street sign, touched the stalk with his left hand to switch on the indicator lights, looked in his mirror and turned right. He then looked out for the house numbers. He wanted 111. The first house was 2, so he was looking on the even side. On his right there was number 9. That's better. It was a long road. He put his foot on the accelerator and caught up with the number 93, then 95, 97. And reached a T junction. 97 looked like the last house on the right hand side. He slowed down, pulled into the near side and stopped the car. He got out. Looked up at the last number on the even number side. It was 98. He crossed the pavement, opened the gate, went up two steps and pressed the doorbell.

A woman came to the door. She looked at him and smiled.

He raised his hat and said, 'I am sorry to bother you. I am looking for number 111 Brook Street.'

'Sorry, love. The isn't a 111. Are you sure it isn't just number 11?'

Angel frowned.

'You see the numbers stop here. This is number 98. Who are you wanting? Maybe I know her.'

'It's a Mr Jameson, actually.'

'No, I've never heard of him, love. Are you sure you don't want number 11.'

Angel thanked her.

The door closed.

He came down the steps with a pained expression. He slumped back in the car and slammed the door. He tried number 11 and the woman there said that she had never heard of Jameson. So Angel knew it was a prepared non-existent address. That was the hall mark of a crook. He couldn't wait to get back to the station to collect the laptop with the photographs of the rogues gallery, villains roaming around free and wanted by the police.

He raced back to the station, snatched up the laptop from the table in his office then sped back to the hospital to the A & E department. He had to wait a few minutes in the corridor, but eventually Nurse Naomi Jacobs came across to him smiling.

'You are soon back, Inspector.'

'I've brought you our rogues' gallery,' he said, indicating the case he was carrying under his arm.

'Oh?' Nurse Jacobs said, directing him into a cubicle. 'Never seen a rogues' gallery. It should be interesting.'

Angel didn't think so. He zipped open the case, took out the laptop, put it on the bed and quickly loaded up the programme. Most pages showed a full length photograph of a man, with an inset close up photograph of his head, showing him looking to the front and another to his side. The photographs were mostly taken in prison the day the prisoner arrived there. Some others were much more haphazard, and taken from a car, or on the street or from some under cover surveillance.

'Will you look at each photograph?' Angel said. 'And tell me if you see anybody you know.'

It didn't take her long to pick out the prison photograph of Mick MacBride.

'Are you sure,' Angel said.

'Positive,' she said.

Angel nodded knowingly. 'Thank you very much indeed,' he said.

She smiled. 'It's nothing. I must get back,' she said and she dashed off.

Angel's face turned to a frown. He now had another puzzle. What does the mighty MacBride want at the Monks' Retreat?

He thanked Nurse Jacobs, closed up the laptop, returned to the BMW and drove it straight across the moors to the small market town of Tunistone. Two miles from there, off a side road which was itself off the main Manchester road was the Monks' Retreat. It was in the middle of nowhere.

Angel knew exactly where it was although he had never been inside. He remembered the big wooden gates and the pokerwork sign. The gates had always been closed whenever he had passed. Today they were wide open.

He drove straight in and followed the grey gravel round to what appeared to be the front of the house. He spotted a big door with three stone steps leading up to it. He drove the BMW slowly towards it and stopped.

At that very same moment, Mrs Buller-Price opened the front door. She came outside surrounded by her three dogs and closed the door. She saw the car and Angel climbing out of it and beamed.

'How very nice to see you, Inspector,' she said.

The dogs rushed over to smell and survey him. He stopped a few yards from the door, leaned forward and put his hands out for them to sniff at and lick.

'I've come over to see how you are and, if you will allow me, a look over the place.'

'Of course, and you are most welcome.' She turned back to the door. 'I was just taking the dogs for a short walk round the lake, but come in.'

'I'd love a bit of fresh air. I'll join you, if you'll have me. And perhaps you can show me where you found that little plaque?'

'Certainly. With pleasure. It was at the far end of the lake. Come along then. I remember exactly where it was.'

They pressed forward. Mrs Buller-Price leading the way and Angel at her side.

The dogs rushed ahead chasing real or imaginary birds. From time to time, they picked up a scent and followed something for a little while, then nosed around in the grass and wild flowers sniffing at what was evidently its destination.

'Did your scientists make anything of that . . . that torn piece of cloth?'

He thought quickly. He didn't want to alarm her.

'Only that it came from the pants of a trespasser,' he said.

They pressed forward enjoying the fresh air and the gentle lapping of the water in the lake only several metres away.

When they were at the far end of the lake, Mrs Buller-Price stopped and pointed to a place in the grass. 'Bogart found the plaque just there,' she said.

Angel crouched down at the spot and looked around the grass. On his right was the lake about a metre away and to his left through the trees and bushes he could just see the stone boundary wall about thirty metres away. He stood up and walked across the strip of grass, around the trees and bushes to the wall, which at that point was about one and half metres high. He looked over the wall and spotted convenient footholds between the stones. He saw that the wall was around three metres high on the other side, also, close to the wall in the mud, he saw tyre tracks. His eyes narrowed. He rubbed his cheek hard with his fingers several times slowly. Those tracks could have been made by a farmer's vehicle. But he couldn't believe it would have been necessary for it to have stopped so near the wall.

'Have you found anything interesting, Inspector,' Mrs Buller-Price called.

He considered his reply then said, 'Yes, moorland, lots of land, for miles and miles, either ploughed and seeded or fallow, or simply moorland.'

She smiled.

He climbed up and the two of them continued their walk round the other side of the lake back to the house. She showed him round the house including the rooms on both floors at the back of the house not occupied by her.

He couldn't find any signs of recent activity. He checked every window. The catches were appropriately in the locked position, except one in a room downstairs at the back of the building near to the back door. He turned to Mrs Buller-Price.

'Did you want this window unlocked for any reason?' he said.

'No,' she said.

'I'll lock it then,' he said.

Then he went down the passage towards the back door and noticed, at eye level, a board screwed to the wall with electric fuse boxes, with mains switches and the meter fixed to it.

He then checked the back door. It was locked. He was pleased about that. He turned to Mrs Buller-Price. 'Have you the key?'

From her coat pocket she produced a bunch of keys. 'I don't actually use it,' she said as she selected the largest one and passed the bunch to him holding that particular one. 'I avoid coming into the unused part of the house. It seems so . . . unfriendly.'

He pushed it in the lock, turned it and opened the door. He peered outside. There was a large surface made of hundreds of old bricks laid side by side. The brick surface extended up to the high stone boundary wall thirty metres or so away.

He squatted down looking for footprints. Nothing. He reasoned that if there had been any prints, they would have been washed away by the recent heavy rains. He stood up. His lips tightened. He ran a hand through his hair.

He closed the door, locked it, turned to Mrs Buller-Price, handed her the bunch of keys and said, 'Is this the only key for this door?'

'I really don't know, Inspector. I only have the one.'

He nodded meaningfully. It was easy to see how the power had been cut for those few hours last Sunday evening. It would have been by executed by Mick MacBride or one of his gang. And it would have been done to keep Mrs Buller-Price from observing whatever it was they were up to.

Angel was even more determined to put MacBride behind bars. The man was a waste of humanity.

Angel managed, with difficulty, to break away from Mrs Buller-Price who insisted that he had a cup of tea and two helpings of gooseberry fool and cream before he went. Also, that he took with him, two thick slices of her Battenberg cake carefully wrapped in greaseproof paper. She said that they were for himself and Mary. He thanked her most graciously, shook her hand and dashed out of the house to the BMW.

It was five minutes to five.

He drove the BMW for about a mile, stopped in a passing place, took out his mobile and scrolled down to SOCO and clicked on it.

Taylor soon answered.

'Ah, Don,' Angel said into the mouthpiece. 'I've a job for you . . . and it has to be done tonight.'

Taylor wasn't pleased. 'Tonight, sir?' he said.

'It won't take long but it is up at Tunistone. I want you to make plaster casts of several tyre marks in dried mud, before it rains.'

TEN

Angel bounced into his office the following morning immediately followed by Cassie Jagger. She was holding several A4 sheets of paper.

'Morning, sir,' she said.

'Come in, Cassie. Good morning,' Angel said as he took off his coat and hat and hung them up. He raised his eyebrows, pointed to the papers in her hand and said, 'What's this?'

Cassie stuck out her chest and said, 'List of calls made on Sarah Steadman's mobile, and those made on the landline at the house she shared with her mother, for the last four weeks, sir.'

'Ah yes,' he said, taking the papers. 'You checked every call?'

'Yes, sir. And there was nothing unusual about the people they called. The calls on the landline were mostly to shops or stores. There were no what you might call personal calls to friends or relations. There were a few on Sarah Steadman's mobile to her GP and to the hospital, and quite a few to the landline. They would be back to her mother. Apart from them, there were no other personal calls.'

Angel glanced quickly at the four sheets of paper and put them down on the pile of others on the desk. Then he lowered his eyelids as he absorbed what she was saying. After a moment he said, 'Who was the GP she was phoning?'

'Doctor Young, sir. He has a practice down Ashdown Road, sir.'

He wrote it down on a pad on the desk.

As he was writing, the cadet said, 'Is the investigation going well, sir?'

Angel frowned and said, 'Who wants to know?'

'I do, sir,' she said.

Angel put down his pen and looked at her.

'I wondered why Mr Stone is being investigated, sir,' she said. 'I mean . . . what is he suspected of?'

'The murder of six people, Cassie. Isn't that reason enough?'

'Of course, sir. I didn't know that you had sufficient evidence.'

'We haven't, Cassie, not yet. But he has a wound to a finger that matches up with evidence that Arrowsmith had a finger bandaged when he was in hospital. He has no alibi for the time that the most recent victim, Hobbs was murdered. And he has a prison record. A lot more work would be required to strengthen the case against him, if we decided that it was worthwhile to proceed.'

Angel looked up at her. The movement of her eyes told him that she was thinking.

He smiled. 'Anything else?' he said.

'Oh no, sir,' she said. She was elated that he had given her such a detailed reply. She felt privileged.

'Now I want you to push off now, Cassie, and find DS Crisp, and have him report to me immediately.'

'Right, sir,' she said.

As she went out, DS Taylor came in. He was all smiles. In his hands he had two white plaster casts, each about as big as a thousand page police manual. 'These are the casts from last night, sir. We have the size and tread of two actual wheels, if we get a suspect thief with a van or a lorry.'

'Great stuff, Don.'

* * *

There was a knock on the door.

'Come in,' Angel said.

He looked up. It was DS Crisp.

Crisp licked his lips, then brought a hand up to his face. He rubbed his jaw, ran his fingers round to an ear, fingered the lobe of the ear, and said, 'You wanted me, sir?'

Angel noticed his demeanour. 'Yes. Come in. Sit down. How are getting on finding Mick MacBride?'

'Not very well, sir,' Crisp said as he shook his head slowly from side to side. 'Nobody will talk. Everybody is scared of reprisal's. The vital witnesses' wives or partners appear to have been paid handsomely to keep their mouths shut. Nobody in the prison or out of the prison *knows* anything, or *saw* anything.'

'Who have you interviewed?''

'The prisoners who held the gate, plus a couple of others caught on CCTV before the escape who seemed to be matey with MacBride.'

'Loyalty in prison isn't a strong motive, Trevor. Most of them would sell their kids to get out of there. Weren't you able to break any of them?'

'They were too scared and probably too well paid to say anything, sir.'

Angel wrinkled his brow.

Crisp detailed the other people he had traced and he told him that he always received negative replies about MacBride.

Angel then told him about his presence at the Monks' Retreat and the skirmish with one of Mrs Buller-Price's dogs.

Crisp smiled for a moment at the news that MacBride had been bitten in the nether region.

'So you see, MacBride is not far away,' Angel said. 'He may be living here in Bromersley. He must have made a nice nest for himself somewhere local. It's all a question of *where*. And I wonder, just wonder what his interest in Mrs Buller-Price could have been. She hasn't got anything worth stealing as far as I know. Have you searched the houses of his associates.'

'There are only two that are local sir, and I've searched those. Nothing.'

'Did you find out anything about the helicopter pilot? Any prints on the controls . . . ?'

The phone rang. Angel glared at it, then reached out for it.

It was DS Taylor.

'Yes, Don,' Angel said.

He was clearly excited. 'Oh sir, I'm doing the search of Stone's flat, and in the bedroom under the bed we've found a painting . . .'

Angel interrupted the flow. 'Just a minute, Don. Hold the line.'

He put his hand over the mouthpiece and turned back to Crisp. 'If you haven't any lines of inquiry you can return to, Trevor. I suggest you refer to your notes, see if there is anybody you have not seen and interview them, also re-interview the people you've already seen. Inquire from the probation office. See who is currently on their books. Find out if any of them can fly a chopper, or doesn't mind being suspended from a wire for a few hundred quid. Try and ferret out any inconsistencies. Something will break, I'm sure.'

Crisp stood up. 'Right, sir,' he said and he went out.

Angel took his hand away from the mouthpiece on the phone. 'Hello, Don. Are you there? Now what's this about a painting?'

'It was shrink-wrapped in black plastic sheeting. I carefully cut the plastic sheeting to look at it. It looks old, very old. It is of men in a boat in a storm. It's very striking. But as you said, if it was wrapped in black plastic sheeting . . .'

'Yes, yes. It *might* be part of that stolen stuff,' Angel said. 'I'll come straightaway.'

* * *

It was about seven minutes later, at 9.30 that Angel turned the BMW onto the forecourt of Britannia House, an aluminium, glass and concrete block of flats. It was smothered in *NO PARKING* signs and yellow lines. He saw the SOCO's van and an unmarked police car parked in front of the building in the only permitted places for visitors to the flats. He soon found a place. It was on yellow lines but he was careful not to park in front of the entrance and exit to the private car park under the block. He took out of the glove compartment an official sign bearing the words *POLICE ON DUTY*, which he placed on the shelf under the windscreen. Then he got out of the car.

He soon found Stone's flat which was on the first floor.

Taylor was waiting for him. He was in plain clothes but wearing rubber gloves.

'It's through here . . . in the bedroom, sir,' he said. 'I put it back where I found it.'

Angel followed him through the small but airy flat to a small room, furnished with a double bed, a bedside cabinet, a wardrobe and a chest of drawers.

Taylor crouched down and pointed under the bed. 'It's there, sir.'

Angel said. 'Right. Let's have a look at it.'

Taylor eased the black plastic covered picture out from under the bed. The black plastic was covered in a light silver aluminium powder with several groups of shiny fingerprints showing up here and there. That was an indication that the SOC team had found quite a few prints on the plastic wrapping.

Angel was pleased and he hoped that the owner or owners of the prints could be identified.

He shuffled backwards to give Taylor sufficient room to pull the covered picture out completely.

Angel was surprised at the size of it. 'What's its measure? It's a darn sight bigger than modern paintings, that's for sure.'

'160 by 130 centimetres, sir.'

'That's about five feet by four feet, isn't it?'

'Yes. Something like that,' Taylor said.

Angel helped him to lift it onto the bed then Taylor peeled off the clear sticky tape he had applied to the black plastic covering and unveiled the painting. It was certainly impressive.

Angel just stared at it as did Don Taylor.

It showed a small, old open sailing boat in very wild seas with four fishermen inside the boat mostly holding onto something so as not to be swept overboard. It was in a richly gilded frame.

'Wow,' Angel said. Then he bent down and looked very closely at it. 'It's painted in oil. It's not a print.'

Taylor said, 'Is it valuable, sir?'

'I've no idea, Don. It could be. Is it signed anywhere?'

'I looked all over but couldn't see anything. It's usually at the bottom on the right hand side, isn't it?'

'Have it photographed and put the print onto our website straightaway.'

'Right, sir,' Taylor said. He turned away and went out of the room. He returned after a minute with a young police constable with a camera.

Angel and Taylor took the painting off the bed and stood it upright against the bedroom wall. The PC took a photograph then turned to Angel and said, 'I'll have it on line in a couple of minutes, sir.'

'Right, thank you,' Angel said and he made for the door.

He returned to the station, and as he made his way to his office, he looked in at the CID office.

There seemed to be a lot of activity. Detectives on the phone or staring at their computer screens.

Cadet Jagger was at a computer near the door. She stood up and said, 'Can I help you, sir?'

'Yes, Cassie, I'm looking for DS Carter.'

Cassie looked round. She wasn't to be seen.

'Find her for me, Cassie. Ask her to come to my office ASAP.'

'Right, sir.'

Angel turned into his office and sat down at his desk and pulled open the middle drawer. He fished around for the business card left by Detective Superintendent Ephraim Wannamaker of the International Antiques and Fine Art Unit. He remembered the superintendent saying that it was a direct line to his desk. He hoped he was there. He tapped out the phone number and after three rings it was answered by the man himself.

Angel told him about the find in a murder suspect's bedroom. He described the painting then that he switched on his computer and emailed the photograph of it.

When Wannamaker had seen it, it was difficult for him to maintain his usual equilibrium. '*My God*!' he said. 'It could be Miron's *Boat in a Storm*, dated 1636. If it's what I think it is, it's worth millions. No not millions. It's just simply priceless.' Then his animated tone changed. He went on to say, 'It was looted from Poland in 1939, reportedly described by the Nazis as degenerate, and destroyed on Hitler's orders. Hmmm. I suppose it could have been clandestinely rescued. Hmmm. Or it could be a relatively modern copy.'

'It is still part of the stolen loot being landed in Ireland?' Angel said.

'Oh yes,' Wannamaker said. 'The shrink-wrapped black plastic sheeting is the giveaway. I'm coming up. I'll get to you sometime this afternoon. Will you make yourself available?'

'Of course, sir.'

Angel replaced the phone and slowly rubbed his chin. Whether the painting was priceless or relatively worthless would make no difference to the case. There was no question of reward. It was simply potential evidence of robbery presumably by Alan Stone because it was found in his possession. That's all. Therefore, at that time, Angel dismissed all further thoughts about the picture. His foremost interest was on the serial murders. And there were so many strands to be considered and investigated. In that regard he knew he had to interview Harry Simms at Moore & Moore as soon as he could, and he was thinking how he could best organise his time, when there was a knock at the door.

'Come in,' he said. It was DS Carter. She had a report sheet in her hand.

'Ah, Flora,' Angel said. 'I don't suppose Bloomfield is in the building?'

'Not as far as I know, sir,' she said. 'He was with Alan Stone yesterday but I haven't seen him today.'

'Right, Flora,' he said. 'Sit down a minute. Must just make this call.'

Angel reached out for his phone and dialled a number. As it rang out, he noticed the report sheet she was holding and said, 'What's that?'

'Yesterday, you asked me to let you have a list of the all the cars and their owners parked around Moore & Moore's building early yesterday morning,' she said passing it across to him.

He frowned. 'Yes,' he said. 'But I can't remember why I asked you for it. Anyway, thank you.'

He glanced at it, then put it on the pile of paper in front of him, as a voice from the phone said, 'Bloomfield here. You wanted me Inspector?'

'Ah, yes. Good morning, Mr Bloomfield. Regarding your client, Alan Stone. We have found some damning evidence in his flat. I need to interview him as soon as possible. What's the earliest you could make yourself available?'

'What exactly is this damning evidence you refer to, Inspector?'

Angel told him about the finding of the reputedly priceless painting thought to be stolen.

'Let me see, Inspector,' Broomfield said. 'Two o'clock today. How's that?'

Angel ran his tongue over his bottom lip. He was hoping for an earlier time.

'Can you make it one?'

'Well, I'll need a few minutes to consult with my client, of course. One thirty? How's that? Then I can just squeeze lunch in before I come.'

'Fine, Mr Bloomfield. Thank you. One thirty it is.'

He replaced the phone, looked at his watch and stood up. He turned to Flora. 'I want you to sit in with me when I interview Stone at one thirty. Will you see that he is in interview room one at that time?'

'Right, sir.'

He put on his hat and reached out for his coat. 'I'm going to Moore & Moore's. I still have a man I must see.'

* * *

Angel settled into the little interview room behind the reception desk that Mr Moore had kindly made available to him. He put the small recording machine on the desk in front of him, switched it on and checked that the spools were rotating.

There was a knock on the door.

'Come in,' Angel called.

A smartly dressed man in his twenties opened the door. 'Inspector Angel?' he said. 'Harry Simms.'

Angel stood up. 'Ah yes. Please come in, Mr Simms. Sit down. I'm recording this interview to save time and avoid any error. I hope you don't object?'

Simms looked at the miniature machine, nodded and smiled. 'No,' he said. 'Of course not.'

When they were both seated, Harry Simms said, 'May I say that it is quite an honour to be interviewed by the famous Inspector Angel. What do they say? That you're the detective who, like the Mounties, always gets his man.'

Angel shuffled uncomfortably in the chair. He had heard that a thousand times before. It was such a corny line to use to suck up to a chap. It triggered Angel off to thinking what a great time the clever dick newspapers would have if he *failed* to catch the murderer.

'That gives the wrong impression,' he said. 'I have a highly skilled team of experts and a good deal of science to help me.'

Angel was always worried when the Mounties thing was quoted. *He* never said it. It was the invention of a young, ardent journalist who wrote an article puffing him up. No doubt it was in preparation for when Angel couldn't solve a murder case when the newspapers would then turn unfriendly and could then rip him to pieces. But he mustn't dwell on it. He must move on.

He remembered to look at Simms's fingers to see if any appeared to have had an injury recently and had needed bandaging . . . but there was nothing to see, no sign of any injury, spot, scratch or abrasion. Only a big plain gold ring on the middle finger of the right hand.

Angel said, 'Mr Simms, can you tell me where you were yesterday morning between 7.30 and 8.30?'

'Yeah. Sure. I was at my home, getting ready to come here.'

'Is there anybody to confirm you were there?'

Simms smiled. 'Oh, it's this alibi thing, isn't it? Yes, my partner was with me. She can confirm what I say.'

'What's her name and where do you live?'

'My address is 120 Canal Road, and her name is Tilly Proctor.'

Angel knew Canal Road. It was the least prestigious part of the town. 'Does she go out to work?' he said.

'Oh yes,' Simms said. 'She works at Binns the bakers, 26/28 Back Edward Street, off Doncaster Road.'

Angel rubbed his chin. He looked at his watch. He was thinking, that provided Tilly Proctor could confirm Harry Simms's alibi, there was no point in spending time investigating him any further.

He reached out, picked up his pocket recorder and stood up. 'Thank you very much, Mr Simms,' he said. 'I may have to see you again, but that's all for now. Good morning.'

Simms looked pleased. He stood up.

'Great to have met you, Inspector,' Harry Simms said. 'Good morning to you.'

But Angel had gone.

ELEVEN

Back Edward Street was the service street of, and parallel to Doncaster Road. There was a Binns van parked on the street close to the three stone steps that led down from the pavement to the wooden bakery door which was a prefabricated building spread across three back gardens.

Angel parked up behind the van, made his way down the steps to a door and knocked. A suntanned man, dressed in a white vest, white trousers and a white hat came out. He wasn't pleased. He had a dab of white flour on his cheek and nose, and blue tattoos up both his arms. 'Yes?' he said impatiently.

Angel whipped out his ID, held it up for him to see and said, 'Inspector Angel, Bromersley Police. I understand that you have a young lady called Tilly Proctor working here. Can I see her?'

His blue eyes flashed. 'Oh hell!' he said. 'More bloody delay. What's she been up to? I can't spare her. She's on the wrapping machine down there. I'm trying to get this order finished to get this van away. You'll have to wait.'

Angel pursed his lips. 'People's lives are at risk while I am waiting, sir. Is there any way that could be speeded up?'

He stared at Angel, muttered something rude and incomprehensible, turned, put his head behind the door and yelled, '*Mandy take over the wrapper. Tilly come out here. This copper wants you.*'

The man turned back to Angel, snarled then said, 'She's coming out. What's she been up to? Behind with her dog licence? Dropped a toffee wrapper?'

Before Angel had time to answer, he had closed the door.

A few seconds later, a girl of about seventeen, dressed in white hat and white overalls, came rushing to the door. As soon as she stepped outside, the bakery door behind her slammed with a loud bang.

Wide eyed, she looked at Angel and in little voice said, 'I'm Tilly Proctor.'

Angel flashed his ID again and introduced himself.

'Do you know a man called Harry Simms?' he said.

She hesitated before answering. 'Yes, I know him.'

Angel rubbed his chin. He was going to be careful too. 'How well did you know him?'

'As well as I know anybody. Why?'

'I have just interviewed him at Moore and Moore's.'

'He hasn't done anything wrong, has he?'

'Not as far as I know. Do you know of anything different?'

'Oh no,' she said quickly. 'I just wondered.'

'I'll ask you again. How well do you know him?'

'Well, erm, we're, erm . . . he's my partner. Since last night.'

She looked directly at Angel and smiled dreamily.

Angel licked his bottom lip with the tip of his tongue. 'Since last night?' he said.

'Well, we've known each other for a long time and been in a relationship twice before.'

'So how long have you known him altogether?'

'Oh ages. Met him last Christmas. At a party.'

Angel's eyes narrowed. 'Last Christmas? Do you mean three months ago or fifteen months ago?'

'Nah. *Three* months ago.'

He nodded slightly. 'Can you say where he was yesterday morning between 7.30 and 8.30?'

She stared at Angel briefly, then she smiled and said, 'You're kidding aren't you?'

He looked at her trying to understand what she was thinking.

'We was in bed together of course,' she said with a snigger. 'What did you think?'

The muscles round Angel's mouth tightened. 'Miss Proctor,' he said. 'I'm not interested in your . . . Can you confirm that Mr Harry Simms was with you between 7.30 and 8.30 yesterday morning or not?'

'Oh, well, yes, sort of . . .'

'Well what time do you start work here?'

'I'm on the wrapper, so I don't have to be here until eight o'clock.'

'So what time do you leave Canal Road?'

'Twenty to eight. And that's pretty tight. Sometimes I have to run. Binssy — Mr Binns, that's the boss, him in the vest, he goes livid if I'm late!'

'So yesterday morning . . . ?'

'Well, I was a bit late . . . only a minute or so . . .'

'So you must have left the house around a quarter to eight or just before?'

'Yep. Binssy went purple.' She smirked. 'He was *that* mad.'

'So you were *not* with Harry Simms between 7.45 and 8.30 yesterday morning?'

'Erm, I suppose not.'

Angel was not pleased. His fists tightened.

'When I left him, he was still in bed,' she said. 'He couldn't have been there long. He starts at Moore's at 8.30.'

Angel reckoned that Harry Simms could easily have had time to throw on some clothes, reached Moore's car park in his car, murdered Nigel Hobbs, returned home then arrived later looking innocent and expressing surprise and shock.

'That's all for now, Miss Proctor,' he said looking at his watch. 'Thank you.'

Angel raced back to the station and made his way straight to interview room number 1.

There was a PC standing at the door.

Angel looked at him and said, 'Is Stone in there?'

'Yes sir. And Mr Bloomberg and DS Carter.'

Angel blinked. He wondered if he was late. He looked at his watch. 'Have you got the time, lad?'

'It's 13.29, sir.'

Angel smiled. 'Thank you,' he said. Then he opened the door and went inside.

Bloomberg, Stone and Flora Carter were all seated at the table. They looked across at him.

'Thank you all for being on time,' he said.

He took up the fourth seat at the table and looked across it. 'Ah, Mr Bloomberg,' Angel said. 'Did you have sufficient time with your client?' he said.

Bloomberg and Stone exchanged glances then Bloomberg said, 'Yes, thank you, Inspector.'

'Good,' Angel said then he nodded in the direction of Flora Carter who smiled back.

He switched on the recorder, and made the usual statement about the time, date and location of the interview and listed those present in the room.

'Now then, Mr Stone, do you live at Flat 11, Britannia Street, Bromersley?'

'You know I do, Inspector,' Stone said.

Angel pointed to the recording machine. '*I* know. That was for the benefit of the tape,' he said. 'Well, on Monday, 21 March, my officers found an old oil painting on canvas of a fishing boat in high seas. It was under your bed. Where did you get it from?'

'I don't know how it got there. One day, about a month ago, I dropped my keys on the floor, as I picked them up, I looked around and saw under the bed and then, much to my surprise, there was this painting.'

Angel smiled wryly and slowly rubbed his forehead. He looked at Bloomberg then at Stone and said, 'Well it *is* your flat. You told me you have lived there three years, on your own . . .'

'I daresay, but I still don't know how it got there.'

Angel gritted his teeth. 'Did a stork deliver it, wrapped in a nappy?'

Bloomberg's eyes flashed. 'That's a totally improper question, Inspector.'

Angel sighed. 'It is,' he said. 'I withdraw the question, Mr Bloomberg.' Then he looked at Stone and said, 'Let's try this one, then. Who has a key to your flat besides yourself?'

Stone said. 'Nobody. I've lived there on my own for three years and I've never had any trouble like this.'

'You've positively no idea how the painting arrived under your bed?'

'No.'

'Did you report it?'

Stone's face creased. 'I don't understand. What do you mean? Who could I have reported it to?'

'Well it wasn't yours. It looked valuable. It had been magically whisked from its rightful owner and conveyed to your flat. You discovered it. You knew it wasn't yours. An honest man would have reported it to the police. Alternatively, you could have made some effort to find out who owned it and arranged to have it returned to them.'

'Well, I suppose I could have done all that, but I really hadn't the time. And I didn't think about it.'

'You didn't *think* about it?' Angel said. He licked his lower lip with the tip of his tongue. Then he stood up. 'Well think about this,' he said. 'Alan Stone, I am arresting you on suspicion of stealing a valuable painting. You do not have to say anything but it may harm your defence if you do not mention, when questioned, something that you later rely on in court. Anything you do say, may be used in evidence.'

Stone dismayed, looked at Bloomberg. 'Hey. What's all this?'

Bloomberg said, 'Don't worry, Mr Stone. I'll get you out on bail in the morning.'

Stone bared his teeth. 'The morning?'

'The magistrates will have to send the case to the Crown Court,' Bloomberg said. 'I expect the magistrates to grant you bail in the meantime.'

'Yeah, but that means a frigging long night in a cell.'

Bloomberg put on his Sunday smile and turned to Angel. 'My dear Inspector,' he said. 'Is there any way that we can avoid, Mr Stone being taken into custody? I mean, it's not as if he will run away. And you know as well I do that it's a Crown Court case and the magistrates are certain to grant him bail.'

'His only way,' Angel said, giving a shrug and half a smile to suggest that he had secret knowledge, 'is for him to tell us how he came by the painting.'

Stone's face was as white as chip shop lard.

Bloomberg blinked. 'Will you excuse me while I consult my client?' he said.

Angel nodded and then turned away.

Stone and Bloomberg exchanged a few whispered phrases.

Then Bloomberg rubbed his chin and said, 'My client has nothing further to add to what he has already told you.'

Angel terminated the short interview with Stone who was promptly returned to the cells. Bloomberg followed him there for further consultation.

Carter took the tape cassette out of the recorder and handed it to Angel. 'Thank you,' he said.

As they went through the door into the corridor, Cassie Jagger came running towards them. She seemed distraught about something. 'Oh Inspector Angel,' she said. 'I've been looking all over for you.'

'Yes, what is it, Cassie?'

'Oh sir, there's a superintendent with a funny name and another old gentleman in reception asking for you.'

Angel pursed his lips. 'You *must* get their names, Cassie,' he said. 'Is the superintendent called Wannamaker?'

Her face brightened.

* * *

Stone's flat. No. 11, Britannia House
Tuesday, 22 March 2016, 2.30 p.m.

Ten minutes later, Detective Superintendent Ephraim Wannamaker of the International Antiques and Fine Art Unit, and Mr Copeland, art expert from Solomon & Son, auctioneers were shown by Angel into Stone's flat.

DS Taylor and SOC were still working at the scene. Taylor came forward to Angel to see what was happening. Angel had a quick word with him and he subsequently instructed two constables to pull out the oil on canvas painting found under Alan Stone's bed and unwrap it.

As the black plastic protective sheeting was being peeled off, Wannamaker looked at Angel and said, 'Yeah. That's exactly how all the stolen antiquities are packed. Whatever the painting is, it has certainly come from the continent.'

The two SOC men stood the painting against the bedroom wall.

Copeland peered at it and gasped, 'It's amazing!'

His face glowed. His eyes began to scan every centimetre of the canvas. Then he took out a small magnifying glass and looked at selected parts of the painting.

Wannamaker stared at it with his mouth open.

Copeland lightly touched the surface of the picture with the outstretched fingertips of one hand and moved them only several millimetres and back for a few brief moments then said, 'Remarkable!' Then he removed his hand and said, 'It feels like 1636.'

He leaned the picture away from the wall and looked at the back of the painting. He was interested in how the canvas had been secured to the wooden frame. He had a very close look then returned the painting to its upright position and stepped away from it.

Wannamaker said, 'I wonder where it's been for the past 76 years?'

Copeland took two small polythene packets and a small penknife from his pocket. He looked at Angel. 'I should by rights ask permission to take these paint samples, Inspector. Who do you regard as the owner?'

'You're not going to damage the painting in any way, I hope, Mr Copeland?' Angel said.

Copeland sucked in his breath in shock. 'Oh no. Oh no, dear Inspector Angel. Indeed I am not. The samples of the paint I would take would be from the edge of the canvas where public eyes never see. The paint is usually naturally thick there and therefore easy to harvest. Can you speak on behalf of the owner?'

'Huh, I don't know who else there is,' Angel said. 'I expect that — whoever the owner is — he wouldn't decline scientific proof from experts that his painting *was* the genuine article.'

Wannamaker said, 'If the difference in the value of the painting was a few hundred pounds or several million pounds, as this one is, I know that *I* would want to know.'

'I shall assume that I have permission then and proceed,' Copeland said. He opened the penknife and crossed to the painting. 'I don't think it is necessary to remove it from the frame.' He turned to Angel. 'I would like you to press the canvas back in the frame a little so that I can hopefully reach the edge of the canvas from the back.'

Angel assisted the expert. It was a simple process which took only a minute or so. Copeland took two tiny scrapes of paint of different colours and bagged them separately. He closed the penknife, dropped it into his pocket, thanked Angel for his assistance then he turned to Wannamaker.

'That's all we can do here, Superintendent?'

Angel said, 'Are you wanting to return to London straightaway?'

Copeland said, 'Until I have the results, Inspector there's nothing more I can do here.'

'I'll take you to the station,' Angel said.

'That's great, Inspector,' Copeland said. 'Thank you.'

Wannamaker said, 'Michael, in view of the developments, I will have to stay the night so that I can be here to attend the court tomorrow morning. Can you point me to the nearest decent hotel?'

Angel was pleased to have him aboard. He thought he would be useful tomorrow in the court as a witness. 'I certainly can,' Angel said.

'And you will keep me posted on all developments with Stone and the stolen antiquities, won't you? If you need the services of my office or the Met for anything to do with the recovery of more antiquities, unmasking the thieves or catching them, let me know.'

'Of course, sir,' Angel said.

When Angel had Wannamaker and Copeland in the back seat of the BMW and was on the way to Bromersley Railway station, he said, 'What do you think about the painting now, Mr Copeland . . . now that you've seen it close up and actually handled it. Is it genuine?'

'I am ninety-eight percent certain it is the missing Miron, *Boat in a Storm*,' Copeland said. 'And when the tests on the paint become public knowledge, the art world will have to come to terms with the fact that there is in existence another masterpiece by the great man.'

Angel wondered how the news that the painting was a priceless work of art, would affect his case against Stone. If the man was found guilty of larceny as well as murder, which was very likely, in the eyes of some people, it would certainly take him out of the petty criminal class and give him the rank of a high powered professional crook with celebrity status.

Wannamaker said, 'If Mr Copeland is correct, you'll have to put some appropriate security measures in place to protect the painting. I don't think your Chief Constable would be pleased to have to face a multi-million pound claim on Bromersley police if anything happened to it.'

It had already occurred to Angel and was on his 'jobs to do today' list.

So was his delayed interview with Harry Simms. That was the top of his list.

Angel quickly delivered Copeland to the rail station and the Superintendent to the Feathers hotel. Then he made straight for Moore and Moore in the old building on Inkerman Street.

The receptionist said that the interview room was available to him and that she would ask Harry Simms to join him there as soon as possible.

* * *

Angel said, 'You see my predicament, Mr Simms. Your alibi doesn't entirely cover the time of the murder of Mr Hobbs.'

Simms smiled widely. 'The murder of Mr Hobbs? Why on earth would I want to murder Nigel Hobbs?'

'I don't know why anybody murders anybody these days. The risk of getting caught is so high. You *said* that you were with Tilly Proctor and she says you weren't. I spoke to her boss, Binns, and he said that although she was frequently late, she *was* on time yesterday morning which means that she must have left your flat before 7.45 to get to Binns' by 8 o'clock. So the question remains where were you between 7.45 and 8.30?'

A sheen of perspiration appeared on Simms's forehead. 'I was in the flat getting ready until around 8.20 I suppose,' he said. 'That's when I got in my car and drove to Moore's. I arrived there a minute or two before 8.30.'

'Yes, but you could have easily dressed and left from home at 8.00, arrived at the scene at 8.08, murdered him sometime between then and 8.20, then driven off somewhere returning at your usual time, expressing shock, surprise and horror.'

Simms's eyes flashed. 'I suppose I *could* have,' he said, 'but I *didn't* . . . and you can't prove that I did.'

'I would like you to accompany me to the station to take a saliva sample from you to determine your DNA, and have my SOC team search your flat. I trust you have no objection?'

'Are you arresting me?'

'No, sir, not unless you force me to. Let's say you are coming to the police station to assist us with our inquiries.'

* * *

Harry Simms accompanied Angel back to Bromersley police station in the BMW. Neither of them spoke during the short journey.

Angel showed him into the charge room. Sergeant Clifton was the duty officer seated behind the desk.

Simms looked round. His eyes were cold, dead and moist.

'Ah, Bernie,' Angel said. 'This gentleman is Mr Harry Simms. I am not charging him with anything because he has agreed to have his DNA checked and confirmed. Will you do the honours?'

'Right, sir,' Clifton said.

Angel returned to his office, looked at his watch. It was 5 o'clock. He quickly tapped in SOCO's number.

It was answered by DS Taylor.

'Glad I caught you, Don. I want you to search Harry Simms house, 120 Canal Road immediately. You won't need a key. There should be a young woman there, partner of the suspect. It shouldn't take four of you more than an hour. It's only a small house, two up and two down.'

'Right, sir,' Taylor said.

Angel then phoned his opposite number in the uniformed department of the force, Inspector Asquith.

'Haydn,' Angel said. 'I am wanting four of your lads to provide secure transportation of a big, valuable oil painting from a flat in Britannia House back here to the station.'

'Righto, Michael. I can organise that. It'll take about five minutes to muster them. Would it travel in a people carrier all right?'

'Perfect. I'll follow it in my car.'

He rang off.

Thirty minutes later, two burly PC's were carrying the oil painting in its black wrapping down the corridor of the police station. They were accompanied by two more PCs and DI Angel.

'Put it in cell number 3, please,' Angel said. 'Put it on the bed. Cover it up with a blanket.'

The duty jailer came up to him, frowning and scratching his head.

'What's all this, sir?' he said.

'Don't put anybody in this cell, Constable,' Angel said. 'Lock it up and give me the key.'

'Give you the key, sir? Well, you'll have to sign for it.'

'All right. I'll sign for it,' Angel said. Then he turned to Asquith's men, 'Thanks very much, chaps. The time is 17.45. Now return to your regular assignments.'

The jailer closed the cell door, locked it and then produced a form for Angel to sign. He duly signed it and then the jailer handed him the key. Angel pushed it in his pocket and went back into the charge room.

Sergeant Clifton was behind the desk looking at the computer.

Harry Simms was in a chair in the corner. He stood up when Angel came in. His face was red. His fists were clenched. 'Have you got all you want from me, Angel?' he said. 'You've got just about everything except my blood. It's time I was charged or released.'

Angel turned to Clifton. 'How far have you got, Bernie?'

He turned away from the computer and said, 'I think we've got everything we can do here, sir. Prints, photos and buccal swab. But we haven't heard back from Records.'

'No, and I haven't heard from Don Taylor,' Angel said. He turned to Simms and said, 'You'll have to be patient for a few more minutes.'

'My patience is exhausted, Angel. I need a solicitor. I didn't think it would be necessary, but that's what I should have had from the beginning.'

'Certainly,' Angel said. 'Do you want to phone him?' He pointed to the instrument on the sergeant's desk. 'You can use that phone there. I don't know who'll you be able to get at ten past six in the late afternoon.'

'Is this the mandatory phone call I should have had earlier?'

'You could have had as many calls as you needed, within reason,' Angel said. 'You *still* can. You're not under arrest, you know, Mr Simms. You are here voluntarily to help us with our inquiries.'

Simms seemed much relieved by what Angel had said.

The phone rang.

Clifton crossed to his desk and picked it up. 'Charge desk. Sergeant Clifton.'

Angel looked at Simms and said, 'It could be a report from SOCO, about the search of your flat.'

Simms nodded. 'I hope so,' he said.

'He's here, Mrs Angel,' Clifton said looking at Angel.

Angel looked crestfallen. He pulled a face and tugged at his shirt collar.

'I'll hand the phone to him, Mrs Angel,' Clifton said. 'You can speak to him direct. Hold on, please.'

Angel took the phone. 'Yes, dear. What's the matter?'

Mary was furious. '*What's the matter*?' she bawled. 'Are you all right?'

'Of course,' he said, aware that both Simms and Clifton were looking and listening to him.

'Oh. Thank goodness. I wasn't to know that you were all right, was I? I know you're on a multiple murder case. You could have been shot and laid out dead somewhere. Do you *know* what time it is? The dinner is ruined. I don't know what I am going to give you. Why didn't you ring me up and tell me you would be late?'

'I couldn't. It was difficult . . .'

'Well how long will you be now?'

'Probably about an hour. I'll be as soon as I can. Mary, I must go. I'm right in the middle of it all. Goodbye.'

He replaced the phone, turned back to the two men and said, 'Sorry about that, now where were we?'

Simms said, 'I was about to phone a solicitor.'

There was the sound of the twanging of a harp string. It was the charge room computer. Clifton glanced at the screen.

'Ah, there's a reply from Records,' he said.

Angel and Simms looked at Clifton. 'What's it say, Bernie?'

'Just a minute, sir. There's a page of standard bumf, then it says . . . it says, "No record of fingerprints." Now further down it will tell us about photographs . . . Here it comes. It says, "No record of photographs of suspect."'

Simms lifted his head, then with wider eyes he looked at Clifton and then at Angel.

There was no hiding Angel's disappointment. He looked away, scratched his chin and blinked several times.

Simms stood up and said, 'That clears me, doesn't it? I told you all along I didn't murder Nigel Hobbs . . . or any of the others. I can go now, can't I?'

He looked at Clifton who simply looked a back at him then he turned his gaze on Angel.

Simms said, 'I don't have to hang around here anymore.'

Angel rubbed his mouth and chin thoughtfully. Of course, while the Police National Computer (PNC) system was 97% accurate, it only had records of persons who had been found guilty of crimes in the past. Criminals who had not been found out and convicted were obviously not included. And Angel knew that unless something illicit was found in Simms's flat, he was going to be immediately as free as a politician's promise. It was the democratic way these matters were settled. It was the law.

Simms said, 'I *can* go, can't I?'

'You've always been able to go, Mr Simms,' Angel said. 'But why don't you wait until we've heard from our team who are searching your house? I'm expecting a call from them anytime now.'

'No,' Simms said. 'I've had enough. You're just wasting my time. I'm going *now*.' He made for the door.

The phone rang. Clifton snatched it up.

Angel said, 'Hang on, Mr Simms, this might be them.'

Simms hesitated.

Clifton looked at Angel. 'It's for you, sir. Don Taylor.'

He handed him the phone.

As he took it, Angel indicated to Clifton with a movement of the eyes, that he wanted him to cross the room and try to stop Simms from leaving.

'Yes, Don,' Angel said into the phone. 'What have you got?'

'Nothing, sir. There's nothing incriminating here. Three pornographic magazines hidden under the lining paper of the wardrobe, that's all.'

Angel's face muscles tightened. 'Thank you, Don,' he said. 'Goodnight.'

TWELVE

During the quiet moments at home that evening and earlier the following morning, Wednesday, 23 March, Angel had been mulling over the murders and checking through his notes. He recalled that the murderer's fifth victim, Sarah Steadman, in the past had made an excessive number of phone calls to Doctor Young's surgery down Ashdown Road. He wondered if the good doctor could tell him anything that might lead to the identity of the murderer. He resolved to see the man as soon as he could.

Angel arrived at his own office in the police station, at 8.28 a.m. and went straight to the telephone directory, found the number and tapped it out on the phone. He eventually managed to speak directly to Dr Young and made an appointment to see him after his surgery that morning at 10.30.

In addition, it was the day that Alan Stone would appear in the magistrates' court accused of stealing Miron's priceless artwork, *Boat in a Storm*. The case against Stone was first on the list so Angel had to see that Stone, his solicitor Bloomberg, a solicitor from the CPS, Detective Superintendent Wannamaker, Detective Sergeant Taylor and an escort of two PCs were in the court before ten a.m.

Wannamaker, Taylor and Angel made short statements simply relating the facts. The accused pleaded 'Not guilty' and the magistrate told them what they already knew, that the case would be transferred to the Crown Court at a date to be determined.

Bloomberg asked for bail.

The CPS solicitor could not justify any objection. Stone had not been accused of any violence, nor had he been in possession of a dangerous weapon, nor had there been any suggestion that he might abscond, so bail was granted.

The accused was released on the spot and the magistrates' clerk called the next case. The process took only eleven minutes.

Alan Stone was pleased to be free again, even though he knew he would have to return to the court in due course. He made his way on foot through the backstreets to Moore & Moore. He wanted to report for work as soon as he could.

Angel was one of the first out of the court. He was hell bent on getting to his car in the police car park next door.

Wannamaker, carrying a valise, caught up with him and said, 'Do you think Stone will ever say how he came by the painting, Michael?'

'Only if he believes that it will show *him* in a good light, sir. And I can't visualise that circumstance arising,' Angel said without reducing his fast pace along the pavement.

Wannamaker nodded.

They reached the front of the police station.

Angel pointed to Wannamaker's valise and said, 'Are you intending going straight back to London now?'

'That's my plan, Michael.'

'I'll give you a lift, sir. It's on the way to where I'm going.'

* * *

Twenty minutes later, Angel was in Doctor Young's surgery.

'It must have been four years ago when Sarah Steadman first started with depression,' the doctor said. 'I remember that that was initiated by the young man she was engaged to being severely attacked leaving him in a comatose state for some time.'

'And how did that affect her?'

'She developed a guilt complex. She loved the man so much. She thought that she should have shared in his pain and the damage to his brain and his body. Because that was not possible, she felt guilty. All the logical analysis in the world could not convince her otherwise. I prescribed a range of tricyclic antidepressants. They gave her tormented mind a holiday for a while. But, of course, they are not in themselves remedial. She refused to see a psychiatrist. I could not persuade her.'

'I understand that the man she was engaged to was called Philip Marx. Did she ever speak about him?'

'Oh yes. In glowing terms. She used to visit him for the first few weeks of his hospitalisation, but seeing him comatose and connected to a machine and not being able to converse with him, or do anything for him, greatly distressed her. She persisted in visiting him several times a week. It was doing neither of them any good. I eventually convinced her of that and she agreed to stay away until he came out of the coma.'

'And what happened then?'

'I don't actually know, Inspector. I haven't seen her for the last year or so.'

'Maybe she took your advice.'

The doctor's account caused Angel to understand that prior to the assault on Philip Marx's head and face outside Moore & Moore's, that he and Sarah Steadman were seriously in love. Marx must have taken a real beating, particularly round the head. That's what must have damaged his brain. After the assault, he changed dramatically.

Angel thanked the doctor, took his leave, came outside and got into the car. He stared through the windscreen at nothing in particular. He desperately wanted to know which employee of Moore & Moore was the real Philip Marx, the murderer. He had studiously reduced it to two. He reckoned it had to be or Alan Stone or Harry Simms. He knew that Sybil Roberts had said that Tracey Thorne had noticed that Marx aka Arrowsmith had had a finger bandaged. He knew that Stone had a red scar on the middle finger of his right hand. While Harry Simms had no apparent injury to any of his fingers. In fact he was wearing a plain gold ring.

But was that sufficient to charge Stone with murder?

He started up the car engine and went back to the station.

* * *

It was seven a.m. the following morning, Thursday, 24 March.

Mrs Buller-Price's bedside alarm rang out.

She wearily stretched out a hand, banged down the button on the big copper clock and the raucous racket stopped.

The sun's rays shone brightly through the window into the bedroom. It was a most beautiful day for March and filled her heart with joy.

She pushed herself up the bed to a sitting position. She saw the painted flowers on the oblong of wallpaper opposite brightly illuminated by the sun and was thinking, what she should to do with that glorious day. There weren't many truly glorious days in a year, and this was probably the first in 2016.

She whipped back the bedclothes, swivelled round, put her legs down and her feet into the slippers. Then she reached behind the bedside cupboard and took out an old back scratcher, adapted by her late husband from a toasting fork and a wooden salad server. She fervently applied it to those places it was impossible to reach. The 'ah' and the 'ooh' sounds she made indicated that she was right on target.

An hour later she pulled on her old leather waders, collected her Hardy fishing rod in its canvas carrying case and her willow basket of tackle from the hallstand, and went outside into the sunshine. The dogs surrounded her with Bogart yapping and rapidly rotating his tail as if it was an aeroplane propeller.

She looked at the view in front of her. The lake was as still and quiet as a child asleep. She couldn't believe her good fortune.

She walked round the lake to the farthest point from the house. She had previously spotted a shallow point where she thought under foot would be firm and gradual so that she would be able to walk into the water to the depth that suited her without slipping.

She assembled her rod and line and stepped gingerly into the water. She waded to a place that seemed secure underfoot. She saw that the level of the water was a few centimetres below the top of the waders, which she considered was a wholly safe and satisfactory depth for her to be. She cast her line towards the lake. It was a good throw. She was delighted that she had not lost her touch. She waited for the float to show itself and bounce then settled herself for the possibility of a bite.

She hoped to catch perch or pike or trout, but thought she might have to be content with stickleback or minnow. Trout would be good. She would steam it for supper.

The sun was beating down, the sky was a perfect blue and there was no wind. Her feet and back were cold, but she enjoyed the warm sun on her hands and face.

She waited about half an hour and the float hadn't bounced once. She reeled in the line, looked at the bait. She thought that some small breed might have nibbled at it otherwise it was all right. She was pleased. She cast her line back into the lake. It seemed to be another good cast. She tightened the line a little and waited for the float to pop up. She waited. It didn't show itself. She frowned. It meant that the weight or the hook was caught in something . . . usually tree roots or weeds. She reeled in the line. It tightened. The rod began to bend into the water. She tugged hard. She tugged harder. It would not budge. Whatever was holding the line was not a fish or anything alive because there was no flexibility in the tightness of the line. She needed to be certain of that. She didn't want a fish swimming away with her valuable rod and reel. She locked the reel, released the rod into the water where she knew it would float and then waded back to the bank.

The dogs rushed up to her to see what was happening. She walked the length of the lake the dogs following. She went past the front of the house to the little boat house. She opened the doors and stepped down into the boat. The three dogs joined her. Because of his size and weight, when Schwarzenegger jumped down into the boat, he caused it to rock a great deal. He stood up, looked up, sniffed and swayed with it uncertainly from side to side.

'Schwarzenegger,' she said. 'Settle down.'

He barked loudly back at her and stubbornly remained there standing as the boat rocked.

Her eyes flashed. 'Schwarzenegger! Settle down!'

She then picked up one of the oars and used it to push against the side of the boat house to propel the boat out into the open water.

Schwarzenegger barked again then turned round through 360 degrees to begin to find a place to settle. The movement caused the little boat to rock again. It was at that point, that the big dog wanted no more of it. He leaped over the side of the boat and splashed into the lake.

The push off with his back legs set the boat rocking wildly. Mrs Buller-Price's heart beat like a tom-tom.

'Schwarzenegger!' she snapped.

Zsa Zsa and Bogart barked as they swayed from one side to the other and back.

Mrs Buller-Price held the oars in the water to help steady the little boat. She watched Schwarzenegger's head on the surface of the water swimming towards the bank. She was quite concerned about him. She had never seen him in water before and didn't know if he could swim. Eventually she was relieved to see him find a place where he could climb onto the bank.

It was then that she began rowing in earnest towards the far end of the lake.

She saw Schwarzenegger on the bank heave himself out of the water taking a gallon or two with him. The water ran off him quickly. He shook himself and was soon bouncing round on the edge of the lake following the boat's progress on dry land. It pleased her to see him cavorting to and fro in the sunshine.

In several minutes she arrived at the spot where she had had to leave her Hardy rod floating in the water. She lifted it out by the handle and wound in as much line as she could. Then she locked the reel, put the rod to dry out across the stern of the boat, and began pulling up the line by hand. She made little progress, so she peered down into the lake. The water was clear for about a metre, after that she saw a dark outline. It was a huge black lump of something with a square corner sticking out of it. It clearly wasn't a tree root or a clump of weed. She took one of the oars out of its rowlock and pushed it business end into the black lump. It was huge. Whatever it touched it sent the entire mass deeper into the water but when she withdrew the oar, the enormous thing floated upwards until it was only fifty or sixty centimetres from the surface. She could faintly see it. She put the oar safely inside the boat then rolled up the sleeve of her jacket and reached down into the water. She felt around until she touched something. She thought it was string netting about three centimetre squares. She put her fingers through it, closed her hand into a fist and pulled. She managed to pull the netting up to the surface of the water but she couldn't pull it any further. She looked down at the netting and through it she saw black shapes of items that were partly round like kettles as well as much larger shapes with square corners. She put her other hand onto another part of the netting, and with both hands tried once more to lift the net and contents out of the water. But it was no good. It was too heavy for her.

Reluctantly she let go of the netting, shook her hands of water, turned away from the side of the boat and reached into the back pocket of her jeans for a quarter bottle of Hennessey's. She unscrewed the top, took a swig and then another, looked at the small drop remaining in the bottle, pursed her lips, then screwed the top back on and returned it to her hip pocket. Then she produced one of her late husband's spotlessly white linen handkerchiefs, patted her lips then wiped her wet hands on it.

Then she pursed her lips, tapped her temple gently with her fingertips a few times, then her face brightened. She reached over for her fishing tackle basket made from the willow and with leather hinges. She opened it, dug deep and found a Swiss army penknife which had a small brightly coloured yellow float tied to it. She opened the biggest blade and returned to the string netting. She managed to raise the netting to a few centimetres under the surface of the water and began to cut it. She managed a cut of almost a metre long. Then she reached into the net. The first thing her fingers touched was round like a cup or a vase covered with thin black plastic sheeting sealed with Sellotape. She pulled it out of the net, shook off the water then tore off the plastic cover and revealed a beautiful ornamented silver chalice. Mrs Buller-Price knew her silver, and she knew that what she was holding was solid silver, quite heavy and very old. She fished around inside the netting for a while, but couldn't actually pull out anything else. The pieces were far too big for her. Her common sense told her that this was a crook's hiding place that she had stumbled onto.

She definitely needed some assistance.

She must contact Inspector Angel. He would know exactly what to do.

* * *

It was 8.25 a.m. when Angel drove the BMW past the front of the station before turning left into the police car park at the rear of the building. Unusually he saw a small crowd of people gathering outside the front door. He thought he recognized some of them. They looked like reporters. He wasn't ready for them yet. He wrinkled his nose, shook his head slowly and trapped his bottom lip between his teeth. He steered the BMW into his nominated car space.

As he made his way down the corridor inside the station he could hear his office phone ringing out. He increased his pace, threw open the office door and snatched up the phone. 'Angel,' he said.

It was a very young male voice at the other end of the line. 'This is Cadet Proudfoot on reception, sir. Sorry to disturb you but there's a crowd of reporters here, sir. They are asking to see you, sir. And they're asking us questions about the serial murder case you are on, and when we can't answer them, they get annoyed. We have told them to leave but they say they have a right to be here. They say that now that it's *six* lives lost, it's a community matter . . . it's getting very difficult, sir.'

Angel ran his hand through his hair and said, 'All right, Proudfoot, I'll come up straightaway. Show them into the front interview room.'

'Straightaway, sir? That's great.' The young cadet sighed. 'Right, sir,' he said. 'I'll tell them you're on your way.'

Angel replaced the phone and looked at the pile of paperwork on his desk. All that would have to wait.

He wiped a hand across his face as he made his way up the corridor to the reception area. At the top, was a strengthened door. It was known as the security door. It was bullet-proof and had a small unbreakable glass panel in it. The door separated the reception office, front interview room and waiting area from the rest of the station.

Through the glass panel, Angel saw the fifteen or twenty men and women with their top of the range mobile phones, microphones and notebooks in their hands, spilling out of the front interview room. He inserted his card into the lock on the door, waited for the click, the door opened for him, he quickly went through and he closed the door behind him and heard it lock.

The reporters saw him.

Out went the cries. 'It's Angel.' 'He's here.' 'How close are you to finding the lipstick murderer, Inspector?' 'When are we going to be told?' 'Some people in the town are afraid. They don't know whether they might be the next victim.' 'We've a right to know.'

As he walked across the waiting area, some more reporters quickly poured out of the interview room.

'What lines of inquiry are you following, Inspector?' another asked.

Angel found himself in the middle of the waiting area surrounded by reporters of both sexes, all ages and all types. Some at the back were pushing. Those at the front tried to maintain the status quo.

The questions continued. 'What's happening? Are you making any progress. Will you making an arrest soon?'

Angel held up his hands and said, 'Ladies and gentlemen.'

Everything suddenly went quiet.

A dozen or more mobile phones and microphones were thrust in front of Angel's face.

A voice from the back said, 'Speak up.'

Angel took in a deep breath. He wanted to be heard. He hadn't the time nor the patience to keep repeating himself.

'This is proving to be a very difficult case,' he said. 'We are doing all we can to bring the murderer to justice. There is no reason for honest, decent citizens to be afraid. We are closing in on the murderer every day and when an arrest is made, you can be sure that I will call a press conference where as many details as you may want will be revealed. Until then, please be patient. I am not in a position to say anything else. Please leave a card with your name, the publication you represent and phone number where you can be contacted, and you will contacted in due course. Now please leave quietly. Thank you.'

A murmur of dissatisfaction went round the crowd.

Angel had hoped he had mollified them. He wasn't at all sure that he had succeeded. He rubbed his chin and tried to smile.

A voice said, 'Is the murderer a man or a woman, Inspector?' Another voice said, 'Are you expecting this person to commit any more murders?'

'Have any of the dead women been sexually interfered with?'

'What is your interpretation of the writing of Judas on the victims' heads?'

'I'm sorry,' he said. 'I'm not in a position to answer your questions at this time. Please leave the station. I will be in touch as soon as I have solved the mystery and have the murderer locked up. Thank you.'

The disappointed crowd began to trickle out of the front door. As soon as the first two or three left, the pace quickened until the waiting room area was empty.

Then Angel turned towards the security door and signalled to the PC in the reception office.

The security door promptly opened and Angel sped down the corridor back to his own office.

Before he could sit down behind his desk, the mobile in his pocket rang. He pulled it out and glared at the LCD screen. It told him it was Cadet Cassie Jagger. He wasn't pleased. He didn't really want the most junior of juniors in his team bothering him when he was busy. His face muscles tightened.

'*What* is it, Cadet?' he said.

She seemed to be out of breath. 'Sorry to interrupt, sir, but I couldn't find you anywhere. You weren't in your office. I tried to find you everywhere. I looked in the CID office, the general office and—'

Angel's face was red. 'I'm very busy. I know very well where I wasn't. But I'm *here, now*. What do you want?'

'There was a treble nine, sir.'

'That's a triple *nine*!' he said, his heart pounding.

'The super's away,' she said, 'so it came direct from the Control Room. A man's body was found in a van on the M1 slip road heading south from Bromersley. He appears to have been shot.'

Angel breathed in quickly and blinked several times. 'Another murder,' he thought, his mind in turmoil.

'Who found it?' he said.

'Patrolman Donohue, sir.'

'Contact him and tell him I want to see him as soon as he is relieved from the scene.'

'I've done that, sir,' Cassie said.

He nodded. 'Then phone Sergeant Taylor at SOCO and tell him what's happened and ask him to get onto it ASAP.'

Cassie smiled and said, 'I've done that, sir.'

Angel lowered his eyebrows said, 'Phone Dr Mac at the hospital; ask him to attend ASAP.'

Cassie smiled broadly. 'And I've done that, sir,' she said.

'And I suppose you've informed Inspector Asquith and asked him for a dozen or so PCs to manage traffic round the van, also to assist in searching the ground around the vehicle?'

The smile went. 'Ah. Well, no sir,' she said. 'You've caught me out there. A murder out of doors hasn't happened to me before.'

Angel breathed out deeply. 'You've done all right, Cassie,' he said. 'Well contact Inspector Asquith and pass on that request and then find DS Crisp and DS Carter and tell them I want to see them ASAP. Then bring yourself here into my office.'

'Will do, sir,' she said and ended the call.

Angel closed his mobile and put it back in his pocket.

He was glad to be alone. He lowered his head. He felt his heart was shrinking. His chest was as tight as the station budget. For the first time in his life he felt powerless. He could not recall so many murders in such a short time where he hadn't found any clues to highlight the guilty one. He remembered that his father, who had also been a DI at Bromersley many years ago, used to say that all he did when times were difficult was to keep up the thorough routine of asking questions, satisfying oneself with the answers, or asking more questions until the truth was revealed. Be thorough.

Be organised. Be diligent. If the evidence is in existence then it can be uncovered. There was no such thing as the perfect murder, any more than there was the perfect murderer. In Angel's experience, his father had always been right. He had to persevere. He gave a heavy sigh, but he felt better.

The man was reported as shot. It was always more serious when firearms were involved in an incident. It cannot be dealt with as an entirely disassociated case, because the victim had the word 'Judas' in lipstick on his forehead.

The phone rang. It was Mrs Buller-Price.

'Ah, there you are Inspector,' she said. 'I'm sorry to bother you again, Inspector, so soon.'

There was always something relaxing talking with Mrs Buller-Price. He wasn't certain whether it was the old world courtesy or the strange naivety that had a charm of its own.

'What's the trouble, Mrs Buller-Price?' he said.

She explained what she had found under water in the lake attached to her giant sized house, the Monks' Retreat.

Angel was surprised and delighted to say the least. He was somewhat disconcerted because it came as he was bearing down on the murderer, but he thought that it was a great opportunity to eradicate Mick MacBride and his gang for at least 20 years, and to recover a stash of the stolen antiques.

Angel had no reason to believe that Mrs Buller-Price's life was in danger provided that she kept away from the lake, maintained a low profile and said nothing to anybody about what she had found. She happily agreed to those conditions. He said that it was only until the crooks had been caught and locked up. He told her that somebody from his office in plainclothes would definitely see her that day. And that he would call personally as soon as he could. She seemed pleased with that and so he was able to end the call knowing that she was contented.

There was a knock at the door.

'Come in,' he called. It was PC Donohue, a uniformed patrolman with a weather beaten face.

'You wanted to see me, sir.'

‘Ah yes, Sean,’ he said. ‘Sit down and tell me all you know about finding this dead man.’

Sean Donohue joined the Bromersley force about the same time as Angel. They had worked together many times over the years and had mutual respect and liking of each other. Angel was to learn first-hand about what had happened. He took in a deep breath.

‘Well, sir,’ Donohue said. ‘I was on local patrol and I went down the M1 slip road from Croft Road heading south and I saw a big, white Ford Transit van parked on the left hand side. I pulled up behind it, switched on my flashers and walked down the off side to the driver’s window. It was wound down. I looked in and saw a man in the driver’s seat. There was blood all over his shirt and his head was slumped down on his chest. I realised that he was dead. It had that word, Judas on his head in red lipstick like all the others.’

Angel turned away, his shoulders slumped, he looked down. He felt as if he had a hot brick in his chest and it was getting bigger and heavier.

‘There was nobody else in the vehicle,’ Donohue continued, ‘and there didn’t seem to be anything in the van. I immediately reported the situation to control. That was DS Clifton. Then I took the vehicle registration number. Tried to find out the name of the owner on my patrol car PC. It showed ‘number not allocated.’ Seems it is fitted with false number plates. I just waited. Then I got a call from your office to see you as soon as I was relieved. SOC eventually came. I reported everything to DS Taylor then I came back here.’

‘Hmm. Thanks Sean,’ Angel said. ‘Have you any idea of the identity of the dead man?’

‘No, sir. I didn’t have a proper look. I didn’t disturb him. Just touched his neck for a pulse. Of course, there wasn’t one.’

Angel nodded. ‘Aye,’ he said. ‘Thank you, Sean.’

The patrolman went out.

Angel stood up, reached out for his coat and hat when there was a knock at the door.

'Come in,' he said.

It was Cassie Jagger. She looked at him as he put on his coat. 'Oh, you are going out, sir.'

'I'm going to the scene of the crime. You'd better phone the garage and tell Norman Mallin . . . that is, Sergeant Mallin that we'll probably need a low loader to bring the Ford van back to the station.'

'Will do, sir. I've spoken to Inspector Asquith. He's sending twelve PCs there. I couldn't find DS Crisp and he didn't answer his mobile. I got DS Carter though. She's coming here straightaway.'

'Right, Cassie,' he said as he opened the door for her.

DS Crisp had just arrived and was about to knock on the door. 'Been looking for me, sir?' he said.

Angel glared at him. 'Have you got trouble with your phone. Cassie has been unable to reach you.'

Crisp looked at him then her with a blank expression. 'I must have been in one of those areas where it's not possible to get a signal.'

Behind Crisp's back where Angel could see, Cassie opened her mouth and her eyes widely, then shook her head to suggest that his last comment was a whopping great lie.

Angel looked him with a doubtful expression.

'There are such places,' he said.

'I know. I know. Listen up. I have an urgent job for you. It's a woman in distress.'

Crisp looked up quickly.

Angel hadn't time to smile. 'I want you to drop everything. Go and see Mrs Buller-Price at the Monks' Retreat,' he said. 'It's near Tunistone. There are valuable antiques secreted in a net under the water level of a lake next to the house. She will show you in the water exactly where they are. I want you to set up two night cameras in the trees overlooking them. I hope you will be able to position them so that we might get pictures good enough to identify the thieves.'

'Right, sir,' Crisp said and made for the door.

'And keep that mobile switched *on*,' Angel said.

Crisp dashed off pretending not to have heard the command.

Angel buttoned up his overcoat, snatched up his hat and opened the door.

Carter was running down the corridor towards him. 'You wanted me, sir?'

'Yes. Come on. We'll go in my car. I'll tell you about it on the way.'

THIRTEEN

It was an hour later.

The weather had changed. The cold March wind howled and made the low temperatures feel even lower.

The M1 slip road where the body was found in the van was one of the exits of a roundabout. Traffic police had sign-posted the approach roads and the slip road to indicate that that particular exit was closed to public traffic.

The slip road and the grass verge had been carefully searched by the team of PCs. They found nothing relevant to the case. Thirty or more photographs had been taken of the body in situ, and a low loader had been summoned to transport the van with the body still inside it to the police station.

SOC men and women in their whites were still working on the outside of the white van. Two were dusting for finger-prints and another two were taking plaster casts of the tread on several parts of its tyres.

Dr Mac had had a quick look at the dead man. He closed his bag and pushed his way through the wind to the BMW. Angel was in the driver's seat and Carter was next to him. Angel lowered the window. The colder temperature soon reddened his cheeks and the constant hum of traffic and the howl of the wind required him to shout.

'What you got, Mac?'

'Very little. Can't do much through a van window. He's certainly dead. He was shot in the chest. Looks like three times.'

Angel's eyebrows flew up. 'By a hand gun?' he said. 'First time he's used a weapon. Are you sure?'

'A hand gun or a rifle. The wounds definitely look like that, Michael. He's not very old. Say 25 to 30. That's about it, until you get him under cover.'

'Have you managed to discover his ID?'

'No. I don't know him and I didn't want to do the contents of his pockets out here.'

'No. Of course. Thanks, Mac.'

The white haired doctor continued fighting against the wind up the slip road to his own car.

Angel quickly closed the window. He turned to Carter and said, 'I'm going to have a look.'

He opened the car door and got out. Carter followed him. He walked down the slip road to the off side window of the van and looked in at the victim. He saw the word *Judas* on the dead man's forehead in red as he had expected. He leaned through the window, bent down to within an inch of the man's dried blood sodden coat and sniffed several times. He could smell powder burns. He withdrew his head and took another look at the dead body, then he gasped as he thought he recognized the dead man. He needed to be certain. He reached inside the van, carefully took hold of a handful of the dead man's hair, lifted the head and turned it towards himself.

He instantly recognized it. His jaw dropped. His heart froze momentarily, then raced wildly. It was hard for him to believe what he saw.

'Look at this, Flora,' he said.

He raised the head again and leaned across to one side so that she could see over his shoulder.

She gasped and said, 'It's Alan Stone.'

FOURTEEN

The low loader delivered the Ford van to a bay in the service area of the police garage and DS Taylor and his team and Dr Mac continued their investigations sheltered from the weather.

Angel and Carter returned to his office.

'The murder could have been done by somebody entirely different,' Flora said. 'The introduction of a gun makes a big difference to the MO.'

Angel nodded. 'That's true,' he said, 'and it's very worrying. We are now looking for an *armed* murderer who is out of his mind.'

Carter's jaw muscle tightened. 'We are going to have to be careful, sir,' she said.

'When you're out making inquiries, I want you to go in twos. That'll give you *some* protection, but you'll still have to be careful.'

'Oh yes, sir. Do you think that Alan Stone has been murdered by the same man who murdered all the others?'

'If the lipstick and the application of the writing are the same as the other murders, I'd be inclined to believe that the murderer has recently procured a gun from somewhere. Guns and ammunition are not easy to get hold of unless you're in the know and then you need a bundle of cash.'

Flora frowned. 'How much cash, sir?'

'I don't *know*. Depends on the gun, but I'd guess around a thousand pounds.'

'Lot of money for a gun, sir,' she said.

'When I was sergeant, it was £25. Even crooks are subject to the effects of inflation.'

'How would anybody get to be "in the know," sir?'

'We know Alan Stone had been inside for five years for stealing. You can learn stuff invaluable to a crook when you're spending a lot of time locked up with one, with absolutely nothing to do but talk and listen.'

She nodded.

Angel said, 'Let's go round and see how they are doing.'

They made their way through the backdoor of the station across the yard to the service building, which was a vehicle repair unit with six bays each fitted with a ramp. The farthest bay was isolated from the other five by an internal breeze block wall, and as well as a big roll up door for vehicles, it had it had its own door at the side for pedestrians.

Angel pressed the button and a PC in the usual white SOC working kit admitted them.

The white Ford van was off the low loader and on the hydraulic ramp. It had its rear doors wide open. Two SOC men in their whites were in the back of it. Next to the vehicle entrance door, was a hospital trolley. It had the outline of a human body showing through the white sheet covering it. From behind the trolley the familiar figure of Doctor Mac suddenly appeared carrying his big black bag.

He saw Angel and Carter and said, 'Ah, there you are, Michael. I'm just ready for off. The meat wagon is on its way here. You couldn't have timed it better.'

'What have you got for me, Mac?' Angel said.

'I've already told you all I know.'

'You didn't tell me the time of death?'

The white haired little man frowned. 'Didn't I? Well, that cold wind through the open van window makes the TOD difficult. I have no way of knowing how long Stone was parked there, and whether he had the heater on or not. It'll have to be a wide estimate, Michael. It would be this morning between 6.00 and 8.15.'

Angel nodded. He turned to Carter and said, 'Make a note of that, Flora.'

'And about the three gun shots, Mac,' Angel said. 'How near was the murderer to the body when he pulled the trigger? Could you smell the powder?'

'Yes, I could, Michael. But that's not very scientific. I'll give you an accurate estimate when I've done the powder burn test.'

'Your confirmation that you could smell the powder burns is good enough for me, Mac. I'm going to take it that the shots were fired at point blank range. No more than a metre away from the victim, unless you advise me differently.'

Doctor Mac shrugged and said, 'It's a near enough guess, I expect. I'd rather see the end of the test.'

'And why three rounds, Mac? At that range. So near to the heart. I expect any single one of those rounds would have killed the poor man.'

Mac smiled. 'I expect you are right, Michael. Why three rounds? Because he wanted to be certain of killing Stone, I expect. He was taking no chances.'

Angel nodded. 'You've seen more of the dead man that I have, Mac. Does the writing of "Judas" look as if it had been executed by the same hand? And will you check very carefully whether or not the lipstick is exactly the same as that used on the other six victims?'

Mac nodded. 'It certainly looks as if it has been executed by the same hand, Michael. You are concerned, aren't you that the murder of Stone might have been executed by a copycat murderer?'

'Yeah. Well Stone *is* the first victim to be murdered with a gun.'

'Don't worry. I'll check on that as I do the PM. And I will let you know if the lipstick *isn't* the same as the other victims.'

Angel nodded. He turned to Carter and said, 'Make a note of that, Flora.'

There was a banging on the shutter followed by a male voice shouting outside, 'Mortuary. Mortuary.'

Mac's eyebrows shot up. 'That's for me,' he said. 'I need Don Taylor to open this door. Anything else, Michael?'

'Yes, Mac. There's a little thing been bothering me for some time. I was under the impression that Marx aka Arrowsmith — our murderer — had an injury of some sort on a finger. That was because a witness reckons she noticed that one of his fingers was bandaged when he was in the hospital having his face reconstructed 4 years ago. Now I noticed that Alan Stone had a rather obvious scar on the middle finger of his right hand . . . other evidence was coming together so much so that I was beginning to believe that he was the murderer.'

Mac smiled. 'What are you asking me, Michael?'

Angel shook his head. 'I suppose, as a surgeon, who has seen many operations, I'm asking you what sort of injury would require a lone finger to be bandaged as I have described.'

'But you have na described how it was bandaged or which finger it was.'

'It's because I don't know. The information came from a witness who was told it by another who is now dead. Nevertheless, Mac, I cannot disregard it. Its source seems to be wholly reliable.'

'Well Michael, it could have been anything from a pimple to a major injury. And there is something else. Because of the electrical equipment that may have been used in theatre, patients are always required to remove all jewellery. A minor wound could be made where a finger ring had been too tight and had to be cut off. Or it could simply be that the patient didn't want to remove a ring for sentimental reasons. In which case, depending on the surgeon, the ring could have been robustly covered to insulate the item from any possible contact with any equipment terminals. There is a lot of powered technical equipment used in the theatre and on the wards these days. Does that help?'

'So it may not have been a wound at all, Mac . . . but simply a ring that could conduct electricity, that was heavily bandaged for the patient's safety?'

'Aye,' Mac said. Then he looked round the workshop.

Angel remembered that Harry Simms had a big plain gold ring on the middle finger of his right hand. 'Thanks, Mac,' he said. 'That might have helped a lot.'

'I can just remember the time when that information would have cost you fifty guineas.'

Angel smiled. 'This is the Fat Chance saloon, you are in, Mac.'

The Scotsman frowned then grinned. 'I'd better get out of here while I've still got my shirt. I must find Don Taylor.' He wandered off towards the van.

At the same time, Angel's mobile rang out. He pulled it out of his pocket. It was Cadet Jagger. 'What is it, Cassie?' he said.

'Superintendent Harker is wanting you, sir,' she said. 'He's just got back. He wants to see you immediately.'

Angel's face muscles tightened. It was very inconvenient. He was thinking, Harker had been away for four or five days on some jolly or other and now he's back he expected everybody to jump up and down. It would only be a pep talk about the cost of something or other. He wouldn't offer a single thing that would help Angel to find this serial murderer.

'Are you there, sir?' Jagger said. 'Did you hear me?'

'Yes. I heard you, Cassie,' he said. 'Loud and clear.'

Angel was still thinking about it. His heart beat loud and his fists alternately tightened and relaxed.

'Have you got a reply, sir?' she said. 'I think he'll be expecting me to come back to him.'

'Yes. I am sure he is. Tell him you've reached me and that I have acknowledged the message.'

'Right, sir,' she said.

Angel snapped shut the phone and rammed it hard into his pocket. He could feel a hot cloud of anger and resentment floating upwards from his stomach through his chest to his face making it radiate an angry red.

Carter was standing next to him and noticed the change. 'Everything all right, sir?' she said.

He glared at her and said, 'Oh yes, Flora. Everything is absolutely *ducky*! This investigation is coming to a conclusion and the super wants to see me.'

Carter didn't know what to say.

At that point Taylor appeared. He was carrying a clipboard. Mac was close behind him.

Angel saw him and said, 'I want to have a word with you, Don.'

'Can I just let the mortuary men in, sir?' Taylor said.

Angel glanced at his watch, ran his hand through his hair and said, 'Don't let it take all day.'

Taylor blinked. He was surprised at Angel's reply.

Angel and Carter watched Taylor as he put the clipboard under his arm, crossed to the control box by the shutter and pressed a green button. The big door slowly opened from the bottom. When it was about two metres high, Taylor took his finger off the button and it stopped. Two men in green overalls came in, saw Mac, exchanged a few words, then one of them wheeled the trolley with the body of Alan Stone on it under the door and outside. Mac accompanied them.

When the vehicle door was closed, Taylor turned to Angel and said, 'Right, sir. Now I'm all yours.'

Angel's face was flushed. He pulled at his shirt collar and said, 'I don't want to be yours, lad. I'm married. I just want some information.'

Taylor frowned. He knew he would have to choose his words carefully. He glanced at the clipboard and said, 'You want to know if we have found anything unusual in connection with the case, sir?'

Angel's lips tightened into a white slash. 'Well yes, Sergeant, if it isn't too much trouble,' he said.

Taylor cleared his throat and said, 'Well sir, the number plates on the van are false.'

'I *know* that,' Angel said. 'Tell me something I *don't* know.'

'Er . . . yes sir. The tyre tread on this van matches exactly the tyre marks made in the field next to the Monks' Retreat,' he said carefully.

'Really?' Angel said. He was genuinely surprised. He rubbed his chin. More confirmation that Stone had been up to no good. He turned to Carter and said, 'Make a note of that, Flora.'

The he said to Taylor, 'Anything else?'

'Yes, sir,' Taylor said. 'Would you like to come across to the van?'

Angel and Carter followed Taylor to the opened rear of the vehicle. There were two men on their hands and knees in the back. They were holding powerful lights and hand magnifiers. Every now and again they found something interesting on the floor of the van. They would pick the sample up by hand or with small tweezers, bag and label it, and put it in a white satchel that was around their waists.

Taylor said to one of the men, 'Give me a sample, Tim?'

The man passed him a sealed polythene bag. Taylor passed it to Angel. It seemed to contain a broken piece of white plaster smaller than a pea.

Angel looked at it through the plastic bag. He rotated it as best he could and found a small flat surface that was gold coloured.

He looked at Carter and said, 'It's gesso. A bit from the damaged frame of a painting. Probably an old frame surrounding an antique painting.'

He returned the piece of gesso in the bag to Taylor and said, 'Did you find anything else?'

Taylor returned the sample to one of the SOC officers in the back of the van and said, 'Have you found anything apart from the plaster pieces?'

The two officers fingered through the little bags in the satchel and one of them took out a polythene sample bag containing an irregular scrap of black plastic sheeting.

He handed it to Taylor and said, 'That was snagged on a nail head that was sticking up from the floor of the van, Sarge.'

Taylor gave it to Angel.

'Thank you,' Angel said. His eyebrows shot up. 'Ah,' he said.

'I recognize that, sir,' Carter said.

They both knew that the torn piece of black plastic sheeting was from the wrapping of some stolen valuable antique.

'Thank you, Don,' Angel said as he passed it back to Taylor. 'Is there anything else?'

'That's all that we've turned up so far, sir,' Taylor said.

'Right. You carry on and do whatever you have to do.'

Taylor nodded and then rushed off.

Carter looked at Angel. 'Doesn't this prove it, sir,' Carter said. 'Stone must have had a major role in transporting the antiques. And *that* picture under his bed could be his pay-off, or his pension.'

Angel said, 'Or he could have simply purloined it, Flora.'

'Yes, of course,' she said with a grin. 'I haven't a mind as devious as yours, sir.'

'You will have one day,' he said. 'All this shows that Stone was not only a victim of the lipstick murderer, who happens to work at the advertising agency, but at nights or whenever, he was a prime mover in Mick MacBride's racket importing stolen antiques.'

'Have we any supporting evidence of that, sir?'

'Perhaps not hard evidence, Flora, but it occurred to me last night looking at his background and history . . . Stone was in the RAF stationed at RAF Shawbury and at RAF Yeovilton where he was found guilty of stealing Georgian silver candlesticks and other things. Both Shawbury and Yeovilton are big helicopter places. He could have been trained to fly those ugly, noisy machines. And he could therefore have been the prime mover in getting MacBride out of Poulton.'

'Well, it's a pity we can't book him for it, sir. The super would have relished that.'

Angel nodded. 'Now let's have a look at this vehicle registration number.'

They looked down at the rear number plate of the van.

'EEQ 7280, sir,' Carter said. 'DVLA says that number has not been allocated.'

'If it's not been allocated, then it's false,' he said. Then he went up close to the back off the van and squatted down. He ran his fingers over the surface of the number plate.

He blinked. 'Hello, hello, hello,' he said knowingly.

'Have you found something, sir?' she asked.

'Incredible,' he said. He raised his eyebrows. His eyes widened. He turned to Carter and said, 'Somebody has been very busy down here, Flora.' Then he began to peel something off the surface of the number plate.

She squatted down beside him.

'They have altered this number plate in a simple, ingenious way,' he said. 'Look, if you peel off two pieces of this black tape from the first letter E, it becomes an L. There.' He passed the two pieces of sticky tape to her.

Her jaw dropped. She looked at the tape, stood up and said, 'This looks like ordinary, black electricians' insulation tape, sir . . . very conveniently the same width as the digits.'

'Aye,' he said. 'And it will stick on all right and can be peeled off in two seconds if need be. A piece off the second E and you get F, and a piece off the last digit, an O becomes a C. There you are.'

He stood up and looked down at his handy work. 'So the new number, presumably the correct number, is LFQ 728C. Easy.'

'Let's have a look at the front number plate.'

They walked round to the front. There were pieces of black tape on it as there had been on the rear plate. Flora leaned down and peeled off the three bits of tape in a couple of seconds. It then matched the rear plate.

'Right Flora,' Angel said. 'Check on the PNC website and find out who the owner of the vehicle is.'

Flora produced her smart phone and a few moments later came out with the name and address. 'I've got it, sir. It's registered to Mrs Matilda Wilde, Ten Trees, 22 Creesforth Road, Bromersley.'

Angel frowned. 'Who the hell is Matilda Wilde?'

'Maybe it's a pseudonym?'

Angel's pulse began to race. It was a very important lead.

He rubbed his chin and screwed up his eyes.

'It could be the hideout of Mick MacBride,' he said. 'But it'll have to wait.'

Flora blinked. Her jaw dropped.

'Get a search warrant of that address,' he said quickly, 'and a squad of armed men in an unmarked van ASAP. Then await my call.'

'Will you be in your office, sir?'

'No, Flora. I might be anywhere. I'll ring you. I've got an idea for finding out who the murderer is,' he said, pulling down his hat. He rushed off.

Flora's eyes glowed in anticipation of what was to come.

* * *

Angel dashed into his office. Time was very short. He began to rummage feverishly through the papers on his desk.

The phone rang.

He stopped rummaging and looked at it. His face muscles tightened. He was on the fringe of discovering the identity of the serial killer, and he had a very promising line of inquiry to pursue in connection with a mammoth international robbery. He hadn't a moment to waste. But then again, the caller could be to give him more helpful information.

He quickly snatched up the phone. 'Angel,' he said.

'Ah! Angel,' the breathy voice said.

He knew immediately he should have left it unanswered.

'Harker here. What the bloody hell are you playing at? I want to see you *urgently*. Three quarters of an hour ago, that lass said that she had given you my message.'

Angel sighed. Superintendent Harker was the last person in the world he would have wanted to hear from at that time.

'I'm not playing at anything, sir,' Angel said. 'But I have a fresh line of inquiry — '

'Never mind all that clap trap,' Harker said. 'Come on up here. *Now*!' The line went dead.

Angel was furious. His jaw clenched. He banged the phone down into its holster, turned and made straight for the door, yanked it open, went out and slammed it shut making the frame shudder and the fire extinguisher on the wall rattle. Then he stormed up the corridor to the room at the top. He knocked on the door and pushed it open. Harker's office had the usual greenhouse atmosphere. But it smelled of mint and menthol.

'There you are at last,' Harker said. 'I'm sure it would be a damned sight easier to get an audience with the queen than it is to get you here.'

'I've a lot on my plate at the moment, sir,' Angel said. 'And everything is coming to a head at the same time.'

'Tell me about it,' Harker said.

'Well, I have a fresh line of inquiry into that prison escape to follow up. And I am making progress on that serial murder case. I have a meeting pressing that may very well uncover his identity.'

'Who with?'

'Sergeant Clifton.'

Harker shrugged. 'Well, he's on the premises, he'll wait, won't he?'

Angel's lips tightened back against his teeth. 'He will. The murderer *won't*.'

'If you don't catch him today, there's always tomorrow.'

Angel sighed. He tried to keep it silent. 'Look sir, I believe that the murderer has stolen around 28 lbs of dynamite. That's a hell of a lot of explosive. And I have no idea what he plans to do with it, he could blow up the station, the town hall and half of Bromersley with it.'

Harker's small black eyes shot straight onto Angel when he mentioned the station. 'Why would he want to blow up the station?' he said.

'Why would he want to steal 28 lbs of dynamite? I'm suggesting the station as a possibility, sir,' Angel said, 'that's all.'

'Oh?' he said. 'Which brings me on to what I want you for, Angel.'

He hoped that Harker was not going to push another case on to him. He had as much as he could handle.

'I understand that there is a valuable painting occupying a prime position in one of our cells. Those cells are for punters, you know that. We're not running a safe deposit box business. Just how valuable is it?'

Angel said, 'We had an antiques auctioneer from Solomon's who said it was priceless.'

Harker's face turned red. '*Priceless*?' he said. 'I can't put *priceless* down on an insurance form. I need a figure. Put a figure on it.'

'Can't do that, sir. I don't know. I'm not an appraiser.'

'Well . . . erm, is it worth £1 million?'

'Oh, I believe it's worth a lot more than that.'

Harker's eyebrows shot up. 'Well, our insurance only covers us for single items worth up to £1m, which means it is not covered for fire, flood, theft or damage. You'll have to get shot of it. And quick.'

Angel pulled a pained face. He had had enough. 'No, sir,' he said. 'Get somebody else to do it. I can't take on anymore.' He stood up and added, 'And I really must get on with my enquiries.'

Harker's eyes grew big. His face went scarlet. 'Sit down and listen to me, *Inspector Angel*,' he said. 'You seem to have lost your senses. I have the responsibility of running this station. You seem to have forgotten that.'

'And I have to see that as few people as possible lose their lives at the hands of a homicidal maniac,' Angel said. 'I believe that I am close to finding out who it is and you are preventing me apprehending him.'

'Don't talk such melodramatic rubbish. I want that painting out of this station in the next 24 hours and out of the constabulary's responsibility. Do you understand that?'

Angel glared at the superintendent. 'Yes,' he said curtly.

Harker sniffed and said, 'Get out.'

Angel didn't need him to say that more than once. He rushed out of the Superintendent's office, down the corridor to his own office and back to rummaging through the papers on his desk. He knew what he was looking for and it was in Flora Carter's handwriting. It was the list of cars parked outside Moore & Moore's shortly after finding the body of Nigel Hobbs. He found it and rushed out of his office down to the Control Room. He went straight to the duty desk. Sergeant Clifton was in the chair.

'Hey, Bernie,' Angel said. 'Where is the map showing where all the Automatic Number Plate Recognition cameras are sited?'

'ANPRs? There isn't any hard copy, sir,' Clifton said. 'It's on line. I can throw it up on that screen for you,' Clifton said, pointing to the white wall at the far side of the big room. He turned to a computer keyboard and began tapping away. 'Do you want any particular area?' he said.

'I want to follow the route between here and Blackwood Quarries at Deerspring, near Tunistone.'

'That would be north-east of here,' he muttered to himself.

Angel looked towards the screen.

A second later up came the map.

His eyes eagerly followed the most direct route between Bromersley and the quarry, and he found that drivers would have to travel on the A1 for about 4 miles and that there were two ANPR cameras located together that would record all traffic in both directions.

His face lit up as bright as a Christmas tree. His pulse gathered speed.

'There are *two* Bernie,' he said loudly. 'One in each direction.'

'Are you looking for a particular vehicle, sir?'

Angel quickly took out the list. 'I am looking for one of these,' he said. His hands were shaking with excitement as he handed the list of fifteen car registration numbers. 'The car I am looking for went from here to the quarry and back sometime between late Thursday night, the tenth and early Friday morning, the eleventh. That was the night of a robbery of dynamite from Blackwood Quarries.'

Clifton eagerly tapped in each of the vehicle's registration numbers on the computer keyboard, then clicked the mouse a couple of times. On the screen came the response: *No numbers recognized.*

Clifton said, 'There's none there, sir.'

Angel nodded. 'That's all right, Bernie. It's what I expected,' he said. 'Now I want you to make these changes. On that submitted list of numbers, substitute the letters F and L with the letter E, and letter C with the letter or figure O, and see what you get?'

'Will you give that to me again slowly, sir?'

It took a minute or so for Clifton — with Angel's guidance — to make the changes and permutate the options.

Eventually Clifton clicked on *Search*, waited a second then the computer came up with a car registration number.

With an air of great satisfaction, Clifton said, 'I've got it, sir. It passed *both* cameras. It went north-eastwards at 1.05 and returned at 2.37.'

Angel smiled broadly. 'Thanks Bernie,' he said. 'Which one is it?'

'The bottom one on your list.'

The fire in Angel's belly spread to his chest and his face turned scarlet. '*I've got him*!' he said. '*I've got him*!'

FIFTEEN

Angel rushed out to his BMW and set off to the Old Town district of Bromersley. He must get to Moore and Moore, the advertising agency and make an arrest before anybody else was murdered, and before the man had blown up the town hall, the police station or whatever target was in that sick mind of his.

As he was a couple of streets away from the agency, Angel saw the car, the murderer's car, neatly parked. Strangely, it was the only vehicle in that street. He slowed down and looked around to see if he could see the owner. He was not to be seen. The street was very quiet. He frowned. He couldn't understand why the car was parked so far away from Moore's, where he worked. He rubbed his chin. His eyes narrowed. Then, remembering that time was short, very short, he shook his head, shoved the gear stick into first gear and let in the clutch. Seconds later, he arrived at the front door of Moore and Moore. There were plenty of places to park, including the company's private car park. Angel parked right outside the front of the building and dashed inside. He came out almost immediately. The receptionist had told him that the man he had asked to see had not checked in to work that morning, and that the staff, except him, of course

— around fourteen — were all in the board room having a company meeting.

Angel walked down the front steps slowly. He pursed his lips. He reckoned that as the man's car was parked two streets away, he must be around there somewhere. But where would he be with all that explosive?

Angel reached the pavement. He rubbed the back of his neck. He licked his bottom lip with the tip of his tongue. He looked around. He was thinking . . . what else was there around there? . . . Houses . . . and houses . . . and more houses . . . a newsagent's shop . . . and the advertising agency . . . and that's all there was. He could see that logically, it could only be the obvious. *It must be the advertising agency.*

He turned and looked back at the building.

He stood there a moment and scratched his head.

He reached in his pocket for the his car key. In doing so, he momentarily looked down. He saw something black and fresh on the pavement. He crouched down to inspect it further.

It was a tiny strip of black earth wedge-shaped. It was black because it was damp. It was on a flagstone near a big wooden door in the pavement. As he looked round he saw where it had come from. It was from between a flagstone and one of the two wooden doors where the barrels of beer were lowered in the days when the old building was a public house and hotel. As he looked further, he saw other signs that the wooden doors had recently been disturbed.

He pulled on the metal sunken ring in one of the two doors, lifted it a little and peered down into the cellar. It was dark. He couldn't see anything. He opened it further. He knew that he shouldn't have been able to move it at all. It should have been secured by a chain inside to prevent entry but clearly it wasn't. He lifted the door to a vertical position. The chain dangled down without restraint from a centre pin in the door. He frowned, rubbed his chin and climbed down into the darkness. It was six very steep steps and he was on the cellar floor.

As he peered into the blackness hoping to see something, he felt a jab in the back with something cold, hard, and round. At the same time, a man's voice said, 'If you want to live, don't turn round. Raise your hands.'

Angel froze and his stomach leaped to his throat. He recognized the voice of the murderer. He knew he was in grave danger. He obeyed the man.

'Now grab the chain and close the door,' the man said.

Angel pulled it and the door closed with a bang creating a disturbance of dust and the flickering of a small light. He squinted and saw a lone white candle standing unsupported on a stone table. The small light created grotesque shadows to appear on the lime-washed cellar wall.

The man jabbed Angel in the back. 'Move towards the far wall,' he said.

As Angel's eyes became adjusted to the gloom, he saw something that made his blood freeze. A cavity had been made in an internal wall of the cellar. He could see the old bricks. They had been dropped on the cellar floor. He could also see the ends of twelve or fifteen sticks of dynamite that had then been jam-packed tightly into the cavity. A piece of fuse cord about ten centimetres long had been stuffed in and around the dynamite and was hanging down the wall onto the floor. The amount of dynamite in that cellar wall was more than enough to destroy the entire building and kill everybody inside, and possibly innocent people who may be passing by.

'You'll never get away with it,' Angel said.

'Oh yes, I will.'

'Do you realise what you're doing?'

'Perfectly.'

'You will deliberately murder the entire staff of this business.'

'Yes. They are all nicely assembled in the boardroom for a staff meeting. Immediately above here. I shall get rid of them all in one go.'

'But many of them have wives, husbands and children,' Angel said, and he made to turn round to plead with him.

The man jabbed him hard in the back and snapped, '*Face your front,*' he snapped. 'And don't try anything clever like that again.'

Angel breathed in and then out slowly. He knew he was taking a chance, but if he was to avoid being blown to smithereens in the next few minutes, he had to think of something. 'You have to stop this pointless killing,' he said.

'This isn't pointless killing,' he said. 'Far from it. Let me explain something to you, Angel, before I take my leave. Four long years ago, I was a handsome man . . . much sought after by the ladies. I could have my choice of any woman in Bromersley; I had a good job with good prospects in this agency and I was engaged to be married to whom I thought was the most beautiful girl in the world. However, when I was found in the street on Christmas Eve 4 years ago, with my face mashed up and my mind in chaos, nobody cared a damn. I lost my handsome face, the woman I was to marry didn't want me anymore, and my job at Moore and Moore after eight months absence was given to somebody else. I was a deserted, messed up, hopeless piece of humanity abandoned for doctors to experiment on. They all had short memories. Very short memories. After this little firework, they'll remember me. O yes!'

Angel heard a click, then a hissing sound. Then he smelled burning. Marx had just lit the fuse.

Angel had hoped he might be able to talk his way free, but now the fuse was burning there was little time for talking.

'You need treatment Mr Marx,' Angel said quickly. 'I could get you help from a doctor, guidance from a—'

'I depend on my voices for guidance, and I don't need any more doctors.'

'Your voices?' Angel said.

'Yes, my voices. They speak to me all the time. They tell me I have to kill you, because you are my enemy. They tell me that you will try to trick me, so I have to kill you before you try to kill me.'

'*I* don't want to kill you.'

'I *have* to kill you, Angel. My voices tell me I must. I can trust *them*. They are never wrong. I can't trust *you*.'

Angel had been expecting a bullet in the back since his arrival. Mr Moore and his staff on the floor above would have been certain to have heard the shot. There was a possibility that the murderer might not want to alert them.

By turning his head slightly to the right Angel could see distinct shadows made by the candle on the wall of himself and the serial killer. He saw the shadow of Marx reach down to the hole in the wall where the dynamite was stacked and the fuse wire was burning. He saw him pick up something . . . it was a loose brick. He was holding it in both hands. He came up behind Angel. Angel realised that Marx was therefore not at that moment pointing the gun at him. As Marx brought the brick down, Angel moved to one side and turned round. Marx missed Angel's head and shoulders. At the same time, Angel swung his closed fist under Marx's chin. Marx's teeth rattled. He screamed, dropped the brick, put hands to his mouth and said, 'Not my face, Angel, not my beautiful new face.'

Angel seized the opportunity. He turned back to look at the dynamite and the burning fuse. There was only two centimetres of unburned fuse showing. He darted towards it. Marx saw him, dived for his legs and pulled him down only half a metre away from the fuse. Angel turned over onto his back. Marx stood up and reached into his pocket for the gun. Angel leaped towards him, head butted him in the stomach. Marx staggered back to the wall, hit the back of his head on a stone, slid down the wall onto the cellar floor.

Angel rushed over to the burning fuse. There was less than a centimetre showing. He snatched it out of the pile of dynamite, threw it onto the floor, stamped on it, then turned back to Marx, who although slightly dazed had reached into his pocket, taken out the gun and was pointing it at him.

Angel saw this and kicked the gun and his hand upwards.

There was a gun shot. It whined as it hit the wall behind him.

The gun flew up in the air and landed on the cold stone flagged floor. Both men dived for it. Angel reached it first. He snatched it up and pointed it at Marx.

'Stand back,' Angel said. 'Stand back.' His heart began to pound. He could hear throbbing in his ears. It got louder.

Marx stooped forward. Stared into Angel's eyes. His arms were bent, and his hands up and open, like a wrestler facing his opponent. He walked slowly towards Angel.

'Back up against the wall,' Angel said.

Marx didn't stop. 'I'm not scared of you, Angel.'

Angel aimed the gun in his direction. '*Aren't* you?' he said through gritted teeth.

'No,' he said as he kept advancing.

'Well you ought to be,' Angel said and he pulled the trigger.

Hot lead whizzed very close to Marx's left ear, whined loudly and hit the stone wall behind him.

Marx gasped. His face turned white. His mouth went dry.

'Back up against the wall,' Angel said.

The young man stared, mesmerised by the muzzle of the gun, edged slowly backwards until he felt the heel of his shoe touch the wall.

'Turn round and face the wall,' Angel said.

'What for?' Marx said, his Adam's apple bobbing up and down.

The pounding in Angel's ears became louder. He glared at Marx and said, 'Because I said so.'

'If you're going to kill me, Angel, I would rather be facing you.'

'I don't *intend* to kill you, Marx. But believe me, I won't hesitate if it becomes necessary. What happened to the real Adam Quinn? Did you read about his early death and his career in a trade paper, and steal his identity.'

'You're the smart arse detective. You work it out.'

Angel said, 'Turn round and face the wall . . . Now put your hands behind your back, wrists together.'

Marx grudgingly obeyed.

Angel transferred the gun to his left hand. He pointed it down at Marx's thigh and put his finger on the trigger. With his right hand, Angel took the handcuffs out of his pocket and snapped them onto Marx's wrists. Then Angel backed off and reached in his pocket for his mobile phone.

* * *

Ten minutes later, a patrol car and three burly police officers arrived and took the prisoner up some internal steps out of the cellar, through the door at the top which opened into the entrance hall amidst the curious faces of the staff of Moore & Moore.

The prisoner did not speak. He looked downwards. His face showed no emotion. He became totally obedient. He was like the walking dead.

Angel followed the procession out to the police patrol car. The senior PC took out his notebook and pencil, turned to Angel and said, 'What do you want us to do with him, sir?'

Angel said, 'Deliver him to the duty officer in the charge room. Tell him that he will be charged with the murder of seven people. And book him under the names of Philip Marx, aka Frank Arrowsmith, aka Adam Quinn.'

* * *

Angel watched the patrol car glide swiftly away then he took out his mobile and rang DS Carter as planned. 'Everything OK, Flora?'

'Yes, sir. And are you all right, sir, and did it go as planned?'

'Oh yes. It went fine. Now Mrs Wilde at 22 Creesforth Road. Let's meet in five minutes a few doors this side of Creesforth Road. No lights and sirens. We need to arrive quietly and quickly.'

'Understood, sir. See you very soon.'

Angel closed the phone and started the car. In several minutes he arrived quietly in the BMW on Creesforth Road. He stopped three doors away from number 22, the house of Mrs Matilda Wilde. Ten Trees. He was closely followed by a six year old plain blue van containing twelve police armed with Heckler and Koch short stock rifles. There were no flashing blue lights flashing nor wailing sirens.

It was a well-rehearsed procedure. The van emptied quickly. DS Carter went with six PCs round the back of Ten Trees while the other six accompanied Angel to the front door.

When they were all set, Angel took out the warrant DS Carter had given to him and pressed the bell push.

It was answered by a woman in her sixties. She was in a blue overall coat and she had a towel round her head. She was somewhat overwhelmed at the sight of the armed police in battle dress.

'What's all this?' she said. 'What do you want?'

Angel said, 'Good afternoon. Mrs Wilde? Mrs Matilda Wilde?'

She peered at him. 'Yes. Why?'

Angel said, 'I am looking for a man known by the name of Mick MacBride, is he in?'

She pulled an unhappy face. 'He's just left,' she said. 'About five minutes ago. For good, I hope.'

'Also have a warrant to search these premises.' He turned round to the PCs and said, 'All right, lads. Get on with it.'

The PCs quickly pushed their way through past the woman.

She looked perplexed and annoyed. 'What's all this?' she said. 'What do all these men want?'

Angel frowned. 'And who are you?'

'I am the owner of this house.'

'Do you own a white van?'

'Certainly not. What would I do with van?'

'Is Mr MacBride a friend of yours?'

Mrs Wilde's eyes flashed. 'MacBride rented the first floor from me for a month. He's only been gone a few minutes. It seemed to have been a very quick decision by him.'

'Where has he gone to?'

'I don't know. He went in a taxi. He took all his belongings with him. He went before he needed to. He's paid up to the end of *next* week. He said his business here was done.'

'Did he leave a forwarding address?'

'No. I did ask him but wasn't sure where he would be. I was very glad to see the back of him, to tell the truth. All those women. He'll get me a frightful reputation. He tried to tell me that they were business associates of his. But I know tarts when I see them.'

Angel could hear the clattering of policeman's boots, the rustle of webbing and the rattle of handcuffs up and down the stairs as the team led by DS Carter at the back of the premises had also gained entrance. Mrs Wilde glanced round and looked very unhappy with the men trooping unescorted around her house.

'Was anyone else staying here with MacBride?' Angel said.

'Well, there wasn't supposed to be. He was supposed to be renting the flat for himself because he had some business in Bromersley to settle up. But girls used to be ringing that bell at all hours. I *expect* some stayed over some nights. Anyway, what do you want him for?'

'To assist us with our inquiries, Mrs Wilde,' Angel said. Then he said, 'You said he left by taxi, where was the taxi taking him to?'

'I really don't know.'

'Which taxi firm was it?'

'Oh dear, I don't know,' she said, her hands up to her face. 'That one with a blue bird painted on the door.

'Bluebird Taxis?'

'That's it,' she said.

Angel took out his mobile, scrolled down to Bluebird Taxis and pressed the button. It was ringing out.

‘I should go and get changed and respectable,’ Mrs Wilde said but she didn’t move from her position by the door.

Carter came rushing up to him. ‘There’s nobody here, sir. No men’s clothes or razor, or any personal effects. There’s a double bed been slept in.’

Angel frowned then said, ‘Tell the squad to return to the station and stand down. You come back with me.’

‘Right, sir,’ she said and she rushed off.

The phone was eventually answered.

Angel explained who he was and what he wanted.

The young lady at Bluebird Taxis said, ‘Yes. I remember this one. It’s in my book. It was in the name of MacBride. He was very forward on the phone, if you know what I mean. He said that he was a millionaire and that he was flying out to Rio de Janeiro for a long holiday. He wanted the car for 2.15 p.m. It was to take him to Robin Hood Airport.’

Angel’s heart lifted. He almost gasped. ‘Thank you,’ he said and closed the phone.

The PCs bustled out of the door led by Carter.

Angel turned to the lady and said, ‘Thank you, Mrs Wilde. I’m sorry for the disturbance. Good afternoon.’

Angel turned away and speedily made his way onto Creesforth Road, back to the BMW.

Carter was waiting for him by the nearside car door.

* * *

Angel pressed the BMW hard to Doncaster, there was no time to lose. When they were on an open stretch of road, Angel told Carter the essence of what Harker had said to him about the painting. He handed her his mobile and said, ‘If you scroll down there, you’ll find a number for a man called Superintendent Wannamaker. Phone him. Give him my compliments and tell him that the painting is locked in one of our cells and will he kindly take early possession of it until its ownership has been determined.’

Carter made the call and then said, 'Superintendent Wannamaker was delighted to take responsibility for the painting and said that it would be collected by two police officers from the Met in an unmarked van the following day before noon.'

Angel nodded. That would keep Harker quiet. 'Thank you, Flora.'

Twenty minutes later, they were at the entrance to Robin Hood Airport. He stopped the car at the first available place on double yellow lines and under a No Parking sign. He put a card printed with the words *POLICE ON DUTY* in the window.

At the entrance to the big reception area, there was a constant stream of people with their luggage and cars arriving and departing, as well as others standing about or looking at the shops.

Angel went up to a man in the uniform of a pilot, introduced himself and asked for the office of the airport director.

They were soon in the director's office. There was a nameplate on his desk that indicated his name was Alistair Morgan.

Angel showed him his ID, explained their mission and asked for his cooperation.

'Of course,' he said. 'What is this man MacBride's destination?'

'I understand it is Rio de Janeiro,' Angel said.

Morgan's eyes flashed. 'That's easy,' he said. 'We only have one flight a day for South America, and that leaves at 15.30.'

Angel looked at his watch. 'It's 15.30 *now*! You've got to stop it, sir. MacBride mustn't be allowed to leave the country.'

Morgan snatched up the handset from his phone console, selected a button and pressed it. 'I'll do what I can,' he said.

A voice from the phone from said, 'Air Traffic Control.'

'This is Alistair Morgan here. This is an emergency. Has flight number 1471, the 15.30 flight to Rio been cleared for take-off?'

'Yes, sir.'

'If it's not too late, it must be stopped. This is an emergency.'

'Hold on, sir. I'll see what can be done.'

'What's he say?' Angel said, running his hand jerkily through his hair.

Morgan said, 'He's gone to see.' Then he pressed down a switch on his telephone console and said, 'I'll put the loud hailer on so that you can hear what he's saying.'

A few seconds later the three of them heard the young man's voice. He said, 'Flight 1471 was taxiing up runway one for take-off, sir. The ATC has instructed the pilot to abort the take-off and await further instructions.'

Morgan glanced up at Angel and stuck up both thumbs.

Angel cleared his throat and said, 'Thank goodness.'

Then the Air Traffic Control man said, 'The pilot has acknowledged the order and hopes for further instructions without delay.'

Morgan said, 'Tell him that I will be escorting a police inspector and a police sergeant to his plane immediately. It is believed that the plane is carrying a passenger who is wanted by the police. We will be coming aboard to arrest him and take him off the plane.'

Morgan cancelled the call. He stood up. 'Come along,' he said, addressing Angel and Carter. 'We must be quick. We are creating a total blockage on runway one.'

Angel and Carter followed Morgan through Customs, Passport Control and two security barriers along a corridor to an open door that led outside onto a runway.

Way back on their left, Angel noticed several planes in front of hangars but the wide, flat and tarmacadamed number one runway straight ahead caught and held their attention. A huge silver plane some distance away was standing in the middle of it.

Morgan hailed and commandeered a passing uniformed man in a jeep.

'Get in the back,' Morgan said to Angel and Carter. Then he told the driver to take them to the plane.

Ground staff were quickly setting up access steps to the passenger door.

Morgan, Angel and Carter went quickly up the access steps into the plane. They were met by a cluster of pretty air stewardesses and a tall handsome man with a genuine tan who was introduced to them as one of the pilots.

Morgan introduced himself and Angel and Carter to the gathering.

'I hope you are not going to keep us long,' the pilot said.

'I'll try not to,' Angel said. 'Firstly, have you a list of passengers?'

A stewardess gave him a seating plan with the passenger's names handwritten in the space representing a seat. He noted that there were three pages. It was a big plane.

Angel scanned down it quickly and came to a *Mr MacMurdo*. His seat was on the front row on the aisle.

He showed it to Carter. 'Look Flora, that could be MacBride. Come on.'

Angel and Carter went through the door into the cabin and walked quickly down the aisle to the front of the plane. They checked out that particular seat. It was a big man aged about 50, but it was not Mick MacBride.'

'Excuse me, sir,' Angel said. 'Do you mind telling me your name?'

The man gave him an indignant look and said, 'Neil MacMurdo. I'm the laird of orl Kinverlochton.'

'Thank you, sir,' Angel said. He turned to Carter and said, 'That wasn't him. MacBride won't fool me. I have known him years. Will you count the number of passengers, Flora? I'll check their faces.'

Carter said, 'Right, sir.' She turned away and began the count.

He then walked back up the aisle, scanning every face. He then went into the business class but there was no sign of MacBride.

Angel went back to the reception area and with a bitter smile said, 'I can't see the man we are looking for. How many passengers are on the plane?'

A stewardess said, 'We are fully loaded. One hundred and forty-eight.'

The pilot turned to Morgan and said, 'Can we be cleared for take-off, sir? We're already twelve minutes behind schedule?'

Morgan rubbed his hand hard across his face and looked at Angel.

Carter arrived through the arch and went up to Angel. 'There's one hundred and forty-eight including six children.'

Angel wrinkled his nose. It was correct. He turned to Morgan and said, 'He isn't on here. I'm sorry. We were given information that he was heading for Rio de Janeiro and that he hired a taxi to bring him to this airport. Come on, Flora. Let's get off.'

The pilot pushed forward to Morgan and said, 'Does that mean we can now be cleared for take-off?'

'Clear it with ATC,' Morgan said. Then he made for the door.

Angel looked back and to the stewardesses, the pilot and the others, he said, 'Thank you all very much for your cooperation. I'm sorry that we have delayed you. Have a safe trip.'

There were some smiles and nods from the stewardesses but the pilot gave him a quick, garbled, 'Have a nice day,' and dodged through the arch eager to return to the flight deck.

Angel and Carter followed Morgan down the plane's stairway.

Angel looked round. The sky was clouding over, there was the sound of plane engines from all directions, there was a small gathering of ground staff waiting at the bottom to detach the stairs, a much smaller plane was taxiing down runway two, there were three other planes in front of their hangars being loaded or serviced or warming up. Everything at the airport seemed busy and normal.

As they mounted the jeep, Angel sighed heavily. Carter thought he was about to say something. As the jeep reached the passenger entrance to runway one, a phone rang. It was on the wall at the entrance to the terminal. A man in airport staff uniform answered it. He listened a moment then caught Morgan's eye and said, 'It's for the senior policeman here, sir.'

The airport director raised his eyebrows. He pointed to Angel and said, 'That gentleman.'

Angel frowned. He took the phone and said, 'Hello? Who is that?'

'ATC here, sir. Were you looking for a plane leaving for Rio de Janeiro, sir?'

'Yes. Why?'

'There's a privately chartered plane for Rio just about to leave on runway two.'

Angel's eyes flashed. 'Well *stop* it,' he said.

'Too late, sir. It is airborne. Look! It's coming your way. It's overhead *now*.'

Angel looked up. He could see it. It was still very low. He had a fluttery feeling in his stomach. He took off his hat. He turned to Carter and said, 'He's in that plane.'

Her mouth dropped open. She looked upwards.

Together they watched the small, silver plane until it disappeared into the clouds.

Angel heard the man on the phone say, 'Are you still there, sir?'

He put the phone back to his ear and said, 'Yes. I'm here.'

'There's a personal radio message for an Inspector Angel — that's you, sir, isn't it? — It's just come through via the pilot of that flight. Do you want me to read it to you, sir?'

Angel blinked. His mouth dropped open. 'Yes, please.'

'It says: "Better luck next time, sucker," and it's signed "Mick MacBride."'

Angel sighed. MacBride had got away again. That would dominate Angel's mind for many years to come. He returned the phone to the airport director.

'Is there any reply?' he said.

Angel said, 'No sir, thank you.'

Morgan muttered something into the phone then returned it to its cradle.

Angel said, 'Can you direct the pilot to come back?'

Morgan shook his head. 'Not now the plane is airborne. There's nothing I can do about it, now.'

Angel's lips tightened back across his teeth. He exchanged looks with Carter, then he turned to Morgan. 'Nothing?' he said. 'You're the airport director and you can do *nothing* to stop probably the biggest thief in history escaping?'

Morgan said, 'No. I'm sorry. I wish I could. If you'd been about four minutes earlier . . .'

Angel lowered his eyebrows and rubbed his chin lightly. Then he turned to Carter, closed his right eye partly for a hundredth of a second then said, 'Right, Mr Morgan, thank you. Come on, Flora. We must be on our way. Did you feel that spray of liquid as that plane went over us?'

Carter nodded and turned to the airport director. 'Is that normal, Mr Morgan?' she said.

Angel jumped in and said, 'It *will* be, Flora. It probably means that they've been overfilled with fuel, and that's the excess. They know what they're doing. Come on. We're wasting our time here, let's get off.'

Morgan's mouth opened. His eyes grew bigger. 'Spray of liquid?' he said.

'Yes,' Angel said. 'It didn't smell very nice either. Come on, Flora.'

Morgan said, 'Did you both experience it?'

They looked at him. 'Yes,' they said in unison.

Morgan frowned, put his head on one side and said, 'If we discovered for any reason that the aircraft was not safe, that would be *very* different.'

Angel blinked. 'Well, I wouldn't fly over the Atlantic in a plane that *might* have a fuel leak, Flora,' he said, looking at Carter, 'would you?'

'No way,' she said, on cue.

Twenty minutes later the small plane landed on runway two.

Angel saw a big red face looking anxiously through one of the porthole windows.

The ground staff pushed a stairway to the door of the plane.

Angel, Carter and two burly coppers from Doncaster station ran up it. The door slid open and Angel and party went in. Two minutes later, out came Mick MacBride handcuffed behind his back with a uniformed policeman either side. They were followed by Flora Carter and then Angel.

Alistair Morgan stood thoughtfully at the bottom of the stairway. As Angel passed him he slowly shook his head and smiled to himself.

THE END

ALSO BY ROGER SILVERWOOD

YORKSHIRE MURDER MYSTERIES

Book 1: THE MISSING NURSE
Book 2: THE MISSING WIFE
Book 3: THE MAN IN THE PINK SUIT
Book 4: THE MORALS OF A MURDERER
Book 5: THE AUCTION MURDERS
Book 6: THE MISSING KILLER
Book 7: THE UMBRELLA MURDERS
Book 8: THE MISSING MILLIONAIRE
Book 9: THE MISSING THIEF
Book 10: FIND THE LADY
Book 11: THE MISSING MODEL
Book 12: MURDER IN BARE FEET
Book 13: THE MISSING HUSBAND
Book 14: THE CUCKOO CLOCK MURDERS
Book 15: SHRINE TO MURDER
Book 16: THE SNUFFBOX MURDERS
Book 17: THE DOG COLLAR MURDERS
Book 18: THE CHESHIRE CAT MURDERS
Book 19: THE DIAMOND ROSARY MURDERS
Book 20: THIRTEEN STEPS TO MURDER
Book 21: THE FRUIT GUM MURDERS
Book 22: THE MONEY TREE MURDERS
Book 23: ANGEL AND THE ACTRESS
Book 24: THE MURDER LIST
Book 25: THE LIPSTICK MURDERS

Thank you for reading this book. If you enjoyed it please leave a review on Amazon or Goodreads.

We love to hear from our readers. If there is anything we missed or you have a question about then please get in touch: feedback@joffebooks.com

Join our mailing list to get new releases and great deals every week from one of the UK's leading independent publishers.

www.joffebooks.com

Printed in Great Britain
by Amazon

59203302R00121